Robbery with Malice

Also by Barrie Roberts:

Sherlock Holmes and the Railway Maniac
Sherlock Holmes and the Devil's Grail
Sherlock Holmes and the Man From Hell
Sherlock Holmes and the Royal Flush
The Victory Snapshot

ROBBERY WITH MALICE

Barrie Roberts

Constable · London

First published in Great Britain 1999
by Constable & Company Ltd
3 The Lanchesters, 162 Fulham Palace Road
London W6 9ER

ISBN 0 094 79620 3

Typeset in Palantino by Photoprint Typesetters,
Torquay, Devon
Printed and bound in Great Britain by MPG Books Ltd,
Bodmin

A CIP catalogue record for this book is available from
the British Library

Author's Note

The Metropolitan Borough of Belston does not exist. If it did, it would probably be one of the so-called 'Black Country Boroughs' that lie north-west of Birmingham; since it doesn't, it isn't! All characters, events and organisations in this story are completely fictitious, with two exceptions.

One exception is the Court of Appeal. No fiction writer could have created that; it is the work of politicians and judges. The other is the way in which a police force misleads the Court of Appeal. That also is taken from real life.

1

'Young man!' called Miss Callington. 'Young man, put down that gun at once! Do you hear me?'

She had gone out to bud her rose bushes, making her way carefully along the brick path between her lawns to where her two favourites bloomed beside the gate. There she could lay aside her walking-sticks and lean on the gate while she paid her attentions to the plants.

It was just before twilight on a hot, still evening in midsummer. The end of a scorching day, one of twenty days of heatwave. There were no neighbours to call to in the adjacent gardens. The heat had driven them indoors. There was no traffic in Belstone Lane. The only sound was a distant radio playing in a back garden.

As Daphne Callington eased herself against the gate to shift her position she noticed a large white van coming down Belstone Lane towards her. She barely glanced at it, knowing well what it was and where it had been. It was the security van from Mantons returning from making its rounds of the chain of corner shops on almost every estate nearby. It crossed her mind that its collection of the weekly takings would be up this evening, swollen by heatwave purchases of ice-cream and soft drinks.

She had turned back to her roses when she heard the squeal of tortured tyres. She looked up in time to see a smaller, dark blue van hurtle around the corner of the lane and slew to a halt right across the path of the Mantons vehicle.

As the Mantons driver cursed and braked, a red saloon following his van also stopped at an angle which blocked the road. The doors of the blue van and the red saloon burst open and two men leapt out of each. Apart from size, they were all alike. Each wore a dark tracksuit top, despite the heat, and the faces of all four were concealed by ski masks. Two brandished shotguns and two revolvers as they gathered around the front of the security van and snarled commands at its driver and his companion.

The Mantons men were not paid to be heroes. Both doors of the van opened and they slid out, hands held high. Miss Callington heard an order barked at the driver and saw him lean back into his cab and operate the release on the rear doors. Now two of the attackers moved to the back of the security van and began to bundle cash bags into the car and the blue van.

Daphne Callington cursed her disability. In the time it would take her to hobble back along her path and reach the telephone by her armchair the robbery would be over and the bandits escaping. She strained over her gate to try and read the number plates of their van or their car, but both were out of her line of sight.

By now her neighbours must have heard the shouts and looked out of their windows. Somebody must be phoning the police. Miss Callington wondered if she could delay the robbers long enough for the police to arrive. At the moment they were concentrating completely on the van and its crew, totally unaware of her presence, though the nearest of them stood on the grass verge, only fifteen feet from her gate.

'Young man!' she called. 'Young man, put down that gun at once! Do you hear me?'

The man jumped at her command and swivelled towards her, pointing the shotgun at her and backing its threat with a stream of obscenities. Behind him the Mantons driver still stood with his hands in the air.

Daphne Callington had been a mission teacher in Singapore when the army of Imperial Japan had cycled in and captured the city. The years of internment that followed had not only broken her health, they had taught her not to be afraid of aggressive little foreign men with guns.

'Don't speak to me like that!' she commanded. 'Put down that ridiculous gun at once!'

The robber burst into fresh obscenities. Behind him the security van driver smiled slightly to himself and began to lower his hands. The movement caught the edge of the robber's vision. He whirled again, swinging the shotgun with him.

There were two booms and a sharp crack that all sounded as one and a red rose of blood and tissue spattered and bloomed on the white side of the van. Belstone Lane filled with shouts and curses and a long high-pitched scream.

2

Eighteen years later it wasn't the third week of a heatwave. It was a black, bitter morning in early December, made worse by driving sleet. I hate driving at the best of times and this wasn't the best of times. They say that the M6 through the West Midlands is the worst-congested stretch of road in Europe and on that morning they were right. As I turned on to the motorway the northbound traffic was at a standstill, cluttering their side of the highway like a huge herd of patient beasts waiting to be slaughtered.

Southbound was not much better. It was moving, but only just. I settled down to crawl behind an enormous container wagon, which favoured me with showers of recycled sleet in the form of a grey-brown sludge thrown up by its rear wheels.

One of the reasons that I hate driving is that you can't think about other things and drive. Well, you can, and lots of people do but they don't live long. The exception is when you've got a hundred miles of sleet-shrouded crawl ahead of you. Then you have to think about something else or the beat of the windscreen wipers pushing through the sludge will put you to sleep.

I thought about the pleasures of being a solicitor of the Supreme Court, sole practitioner supporting an assistant, two secretaries, an articled clerk, a receptionist and a book-keeper while the Legal Aid rates fell further and further behind the cost of living and every day the Chairman of the Legal Board woke up and thought of something else he wasn't going to allow solicitors to charge for.

That depressed me, as it always does, so I thought about Sheila instead. Dr Sheila McKenna, social historian at the University of Adelaide who had walked into my office six months earlier, involved me in being burgled, fire-bombed and shot at, proposed to me, saved my life and then flown off back to Lucky Oz after a couple of weeks to go on teaching spotty Aussie youths the difference between a bodgie and a widgie or something.

Sheila McKenna was the principal reason I had dragged myself out of bed on this vile morning and set out down the motorway. For a man who had spent most of the last ten years recovering from his first and only marriage it must mean something – something to do with six months of frustrating international phone calls and recollections of grey eyes, ash-blonde hair and freckles, under the eyes, across the bridge of the nose and down the middle of the back.

She had faxed me yesterday morning – 'Arriving Heathrow' and a time and flight number. When I rang Australia, an electronic voice told me that her number had been discontinued so I had borrowed a car and set the alarm. Now it was dropping sleet out of thick grey clouds and her flight was going to be diverted to sunny Manchester and I'd have to drive back and find her sitting on my doorstep surrounded by pokerwork boomerangs and foam-rubber kangaroos.

The other reason for the journey was a pink file on the

back seat, but there would be time enough to think about that.

To my surprise the sleet dwindled away, the clouds thinned, tentative streaks of sunlight began to appear and I arrived at the airport in time for the flight.

When she saw me waiting on the Arrivals concourse, Sheila abandoned her luggage trolley and flew at me. We grappled shamelessly and wordlessly for several minutes while luggage trolleys skirted around us or banged into us.

At last we came up for air. 'Come on,' she said, 'we can't stand about pashing here. We're blocking the flow of Arab millionaires.'

As we loaded the car I noted with appreciation the quantity of her luggage. She had not just come for a short stay. She took a pink stuffed kangaroo from the trolley and placed it carefully on the rear seat.

'Ah!' I said. 'The great Australian sex symbol – a stuffed kangaroo.'

'That's a gift for your secretaries – and anyway, all those kangaroo jokes are made up by Pommies.'

'I thought that the convicts started it all. That they had a choice between each other and the kangaroos and they chose the roos.'

We were in the car by now and she glowered at me at close range. I reached out for her and made peace.

As we threaded our way out of the airport I asked her the question that was uppermost in my mind. 'What, if I may enquire, is a nicely brought up Aussie girl doing in a place like this? And why the short notice?'

'Because I wasn't sure it would come off,' she said. 'I didn't want to disappoint you if it didn't work, so I didn't tell you.'

'And what is the "it" which has come off?'

'It's two "its". One is a commission from a posh publisher to write a book on the convicts. The other is a sabbatical year from the Uni to write it. So here I am!' she said, triumphantly.

'And I wouldn't want you anywhere else except by my side,' I said. 'But didn't Robert Hughes write the definitive history of transportation?'

She shook her head. 'Hughes wrote a brilliant book about transportation, but he wrote about the system. What I want to write about is the convicts themselves – the actual people who were transported.'

'Wouldn't that be better done in Oz?' I asked.

'No,' she said. 'The records are here. Britain shipped about a hundred and forty thousand convicts to Australia. Most of their files are still around – a hundred and thirty-eight thousand of them, all in your Public Records Office. So I'm here for a year, at least.'

'Sounds good to me,' I said, and it did.

She glanced around her. 'Your turn to come clean,' she said. 'Why aren't we going to Belston?'

'How do you mean?' I prevaricated.

'I can understand maps and road signs,' she said. 'We're heading for London.'

'Ah well, yes,' I began. 'You see, when I got your fax I thought I could kill two birds with one stone. There's a little job I have to do in London and I thought I could pick you up and fit it in. I was going to tell you about it while we ate.'

'Food! Yecch!' she exclaimed.

'You may have been floating through the skies enjoying steak, egg and veggies courtesy of Qantas. I've had two cups of black coffee at home and two cups of pale grey coffee on the motorway. You can sit and watch me eat while I tell you about this job.'

We threaded into the west side of London and eventually I parked near a railway bridge. Sheila got out and looked around suspiciously.

'What's here?' she demanded.

'Food,' I said and headed across the street to where the steamy windows of a small café showed.

Sheila, despite her figure, has a robust appetite and the aroma of chips convinced her it was lunch-time. Soon we were sitting over heaped plates in a corner of the narrow, crowded café. When we'd cleared our plates and turned to the large mugs of tea, she lit a cigarette and said, 'Right, Mr Tyroll, what's this little job you have to do?'

'You remember Granny Cassidy?' I asked. 'We met her in the summer.'

'So we did,' recalled Sheila. 'A sweet lady. How is she?'

'She's very well, and a lot better off since her husband was murdered, but she came to see me the other day about a problem.'

3

Ever since I opened my office I had benefited from the criminal activities of four families in particular – the Beales, the Waltons, the Kennedys and the Parsons. They were not big-time villains – no bank robbers, no swish drug dealers, no classy con men among them. More a dynasty of small craftsmen, you might say, and their craft was usually burglary and despite generations of tradition they weren't actually very good at it.

One of the Beales once devised a skilful plan to burgle a sub-post office by making a hole in the rear roof. He got in unobserved, he quietly and expertly blew the safe, and then he sat there with the loot, unable to work out a way of climbing back from the floor to the hole in the roof. He was still sitting, pondering on his problem, when the post-master unlocked the front door and made a citizen's arrest

– the glass front door which he could have smashed and walked out of!

Having acted for two generations of the families I was aware of their tradition, but only in the previous summer, investigating the death of Sheila's grandfather, had I come across the third generation back and realised that they were all interrelated. All four families descended from the daughters of Francis Cassidy, a deep-dyed villain whose activities went back to before World War Two. Cassidy had been murdered but we had met his ex-wife who had explained the relationships to me.

Despite the stream of her descendants that flowed through my office, Mrs Cassidy had never favoured me with a visit and I was intrigued to see her name in my diary one afternoon.

She came in slowly, stooped over a walking-stick, but her eyes were as bright as ever as they roamed around my room. She was followed by a tall and broad woman of about fifty, hair originally blonde, now whitening and coloured blonde, who said nothing but was introduced by Mrs Cassidy as 'My Tracy – Tracy Walton, that is.'

While Tracy settled her mother into a chair I busied myself with pouring tea. Her stick placed against my desk and a teacup in her hand, little Mrs Cassidy gazed round again.

'It's not a very big office, Mr Tyroll,' she remarked.

'The biggest I can afford,' I answered not quite truthfully. It always seemed to be more than I could afford.

'Well, you cor say as my lot ay doing their best for you,' she said and laughed heartily.

She returned to her tea for a long sip, then leaned forward. 'I've brought you another case,' she said and motioned to her daughter.

Tracy lifted a plastic carrier bag from the floor and gave it to her mother. The old lady placed it on my desk. I looked at it but did not reach out for it. Experience had told me that plastic carrier bags full of ill-assorted documents were the beginning of cases that went nowhere and hours of work that went unpaid.

'Did you ever hear', asked Mrs Cassidy, 'of the Belstone Lane robbery?'

It rang a dim bell. I had been a student then with other things on my mind, but I vaguely recollected that there had been an armed gang working the Midlands. They specialised in security vans – cash collections and payroll shipments. The press called them the Payday Gang. In Belstone Lane they had opened fire for the first time and a security man had been killed and another dreadfully injured.

I nodded. 'I think so,' I said. 'The Payday Gang, wasn't it?'

She shook her head. 'No, not according to the police. They never catched anybody for it at first. Then years later they had four – Billy Simpson, Freddy Hughes, Peter Grady and Tracy's Alan.'

'They got a long time, if I remember,' I said.

'Only two of them. Billy Simpson topped himself before they had him. Freddy Hughes they let go and it came down to Peter Grady and Alan. They got life, Mr Tyroll, and the judge said it was to be no less than twenty years.'

'Did they appeal?' I asked.

She nodded. 'But they was turned down.'

'So what can I do now?' I asked, sensing the answer only too well.

She motioned to the carrier bag full of papers. 'Alan and Peter have got new appeals in. Since there's been all this investigation of coppers they reckon they've gorra chance.'

I was well aware of the long-running enquiry into the Central Midlands that was producing new and to me un-surprising revelations every week. 'Who were the coppers in the case?'

'Detective Chief Inspector Hawkins – he's dead now.

Then there was Watters, the inspector, and a sergeant, an Irishman, looks like a toad.'

'Saffary?' I suggested.

'Ah, that's him – Saffary. He's an inspector now.'

'What was the evidence against Alan?'

'There weren't any,' she declared stoutly. 'Peter Grady, he confessed, though he said after as the coppers made it all up, but Alan never said a word except that he hadn't done it and he didn't know anything about it.'

You don't get twenty years without evidence against you, I thought. A desperate try by two men who'd got literally nothing to lose. An appeal launched because they'd read in the papers that Hawkins and Watters had been detected in improper practices. And it was eighteen years on. Witnesses would be dead or disappeared. Documents would have been lost. Recollections would have faded. I really didn't want to open that carrier bag.

Mrs Cassidy must have read my face. 'I can pay you, Mr Tyroll,' she said. 'Since Francy went I'm quite well off. I can pay.'

'It's not the money I'm thinking about, Mrs Cassidy. It sounds like a very difficult case. If you want my advice now, I'll tell you – keep Francy's legacy in the bank or spend it on luxuries, but don't throw it at the Court of Appeal.'

Tracy spoke for the first time. 'But he never done it, Mr Tyroll. My Alan'd never hurt a fly. He never robbed nobody and he never killed nobody.'

Mrs Cassidy nodded. 'He never done it, Mr Tyroll. Do your best for him. You always has for my boys and girls.'

I suppose I'd have taken it on for Mrs Cassidy's sake anyway, but I remembered how Inspector Saffary had come within an ace of jailing and ruining me last summer. I'm not a very vengeful sort of person but I make an exception for Saffary. The slenderest chance of ruining him attracted me.

I drew a long breath. 'All right, Mrs Cassidy. I'll read

your papers, I'll go and see Alan and then I'll tell you what I think. OK?'

'You cor say fairer than that, Mr Tyroll.'

4

Down the road from the café we turned into an entrance. Sheila read the sign as we walked in – 'Her Majesty's Prison, Wormwood Scrubs'.

She laughed. 'Lovely sense of tradition, you Pommies. You have royal jails just like the Royal Navy.'

'You should be grateful for a look at this place,' I said. 'This was built because your lot refused to take any more convicts. It's all grist for your book.'

'Great, I can't think of a better way to spend a cold winter afternoon than in one of Her Majesty's jails.'

'If you really don't want to come,' I said, 'you can wait in the car.'

'No thanks. Do you think I'll pass as a solicitrice or a solicitrette or whatever you call them?'

I looked her over. She was wearing a soft brown leather jacket with a fur collar over a white sweater and khakis tucked into short brown boots.

'You'll do for me,' I said.

There was a long queue at the visitors' entrance, wives with carrier bags slowly funnelling into the door. At last we shuffled along the narrow corridor behind the door until we came to a reception window on our left. From behind it a narrow, pale face looked out from under a vertical cap peak that almost covered the eyes.

The Brigade of Guards wear caps with vertical peaks. Among the many other people who wear peaked caps are a percentage who think that the vertical peak is smart, so they cut across an ordinary peak and distort it. In the forces it's forbidden. When you come across a civilian who's done it, it's a pretty fair bet you're dealing with a plonker.

I was. I stated my name and business and he asked, 'Have you got a letter from your firm?'

'What would I want a letter from my firm for?'

'To identify who you are, sir.'

'I own my firm. Wouldn't it be pretty odd if I carried letters from me, saying that I was me?'

'A driving licence, then?'

I drive so rarely that I don't carry my licence. So we went on until I had emptied all my pockets and most of my briefcase, looking for ID while the queue swayed and muttered behind me, and then Sheila intervened and called the officer 'Adolf', and we had to be taken to a senior officer and I explained that she was Australian and eventually they let us in. When prisons riot I'm surprised it's the convicts, not their visitors.

Walton was waiting for us in a small square room with nasty yellow walls and worn brown furniture – one small table and three upright chairs. He stood up as we entered and shook hands with both of us as I introduced myself and Sheila as 'my clerk'.

He was smaller than I had expected, a neat stocky man in his fifties, brown hair greying and thinning above a face that I suspect would have been less pale if he had had access to pubs. His dark eyes behind old-fashioned spectacles were prisoner's eyes that gave nothing away.

'I understand', I began, 'that you and Peter Grady have renewed your applications for leave to appeal against conviction?'

He nodded.

'Do you understand what happens now?'

'Yes, sir. That application goes before one judge of the Court of Appeal and he decides whether we can have leave to appeal to the full court.'

'That's right. If he says yes, that's fine. You'll get Legal Aid to present your application to the full court.'

'You don't think he'll say yes, do you, Mr Tyroll?'

'To be frank – no, I don't. However, if he refuses you that isn't the end. You can still renew your application to the full court, but you won't get Legal Aid.'

'Mrs Cassidy – me mother-in-law – says she'll pay what's necessary, Mr Tyroll.'

'Don't be so quick to spend your mother-in-law's cash. The Court of Appeal is the toughest criminal court in England. It's not there to let people out – it's there to convince the public that convicted people get a fair crack of the whip, but they don't. If you take that court on you don't just need cash, you need a damned good case. Have you got one?'

'I never did it, Mr Tyroll.'

'You said that to a jury at Stafford Crown Court. They didn't believe you. The rules say that, whatever the Court of Appeal thinks or feels about a case, they can't just overturn the decision of a jury. There has to be evidence that something was seriously wrong with the trial or new evidence which might have led the jury to a different verdict. What was the evidence against you at Stafford?'

'There was Pete's statement to the police. In that he said that Billy Simpson planned it and got the guns and that me and him and a man he didn't know pulled it off.'

'But Grady says that statement is a fake?'

'Yeah – he said that at Stafford.'

'And the jury didn't believe him, either. What other evidence was there? You can't be convicted on the unsupported evidence of a partner in crime.'

'There was Glenys bloody Simpson, that's what other evidence there was. She said she knew that Billy planned the job and that Peter and Freddy and I did it. She said she helped hide the loot after.'

I nodded. 'I've read her statement. Why did she say those things if they weren't true?'

'Because she hated Billy. He thought she was having it off on the side and she was. She did it to get rid of him.'

'And why did she name you and the others? What had she got against you?'

'Well, four blokes did the robbery. She had to have four names and we was Billy's best mates.'

'Billy committed suicide before he was arrested. Why was that?'

He shook his head. 'I don't really know, Mr Tyroll, but me and Peter and Freddy were already arrested. I suppose he realised his missus had done for us and he couldn't face it.'

'So you were convicted on a mixture of Grady's statement and Glenys Simpson's evidence. Nobody could place you at the scene of the crime, or connect you with the money. Nevertheless, a jury convicted you. So what have you got that's new?'

He lifted a thick manila envelope from his lap and pushed it across the table. 'There's a copy of my application for leave to appeal, Mr Tyroll. It's all in there.'

I opened a pack of cigarettes and put them on the table so that he could help himself while I scanned through the papers in the envelope. When I'd done I laid the envelope back on the table and lit another cigarette.

'Congratulations, Mr Walton,' I said. 'You've written as good an application as any lawyer.' He smiled. 'Let's see if I understand your argument. You say here that you and Grady were interviewed by DCI Hawkins, Inspector Watters and Sergeant Saffary a number of times in various combinations and that those interviews were improperly conducted, that you were assaulted and threatened, right?'

'Yes.'

'You go on to say that the investigation into the Central Midlands CID has led to Hawkins and Watters facing disciplinary charges, right?'

'Yes.'

'So, you argue, Grady and you were telling the truth at your trial about the way you were treated, Grady's confession is a fake and your conviction is unsafe and unsatisfactory. Right?'

'That's it, Mr Tyroll.'

'So, at the trial Grady was in trouble because of his confession and Mrs Simpson's evidence. Why were both of you tried together? Didn't your counsel try to get the cases separated?'

'He did, Mr Tyroll, but the judge weren't having it. He said Grady's statement wouldn't affect my trial and he'd warn the jury about it.'

'And did he?'

'Oh, yeah, he warned them that everything they'd heard from Grady's statement wasn't evidence against me, even if they believed the statement was true about Grady. Well, that's nonsense, isn't it, Mr Tyroll? Once they've heard all that stuff they ay going to forget it, are they?'

'No, they're not – and they didn't. Tell me about Freddy Hughes.'

'Freddy? What about him?'

'The three of you were arrested. Grady signed a faked confession naming Simpson and you but not Hughes, and he was charged. You made a statement maintaining your innocence, but you were charged. Why wasn't Hughes charged?'

'Because he day make any statement, I suppose.'

'But your statement only said you were innocent and Glenys Simpson named you and Hughes. Why wasn't he charged?'

He shook his head. 'I really don't know, Mr Tyroll.'

'OK, you don't know. Now just suppose – only a supposition – that the judge grants you permission to apply to the court, and suppose that the court believes that Grady's confession was faked. Where does that leave you, Mr Walton?'

He looked puzzled. 'Well,' he said, 'it leaves me not being named by Grady.'

'Precisely. It leaves you with the question of Mrs Simpson. It leaves the Court of Appeal with the chance to say that, even if the police misbehaved and broke the rules, there was still credible evidence on which the jury could have convicted you.'

He still looked puzzled. 'Why would they say that, Mr Tyroll?'

'To put it bluntly, because you and Grady were convicted of robbery and murder in a case where one man was shot dead and another had a hole blown in him that left him permanently disabled. If the Court of Appeal were to let you walk out because a few coppers broke the rules, the next morning's papers would be screaming that the courts are unrealistic and that murderers and maniacs go free because of technicalities.'

'Does that make a difference?'

'Does it make a difference? Listen – the only person who can sack a judge is the Lord Chancellor; the Lord Chancellor is appointed by the Prime Minister; if the press gives the government a hard time about law and order the opinion polls go down; if the opinion polls go down, the Prime Minister leans on the Lord Chancellor and the Lord Chancellor leans on the judges to keep the sentences long and stop letting people out – that's the difference it makes.'

He looked glum and said nothing.

'Look,' I said, 'I'm sorry if you think I'm being tough, but you're in a tough game. You might get leave to present your application, but unless you can prove – prove, mark you – that Glenys Simpson lied, all the bent coppers in the world won't help.'

5

It was dark when we left the prison and the sleet had started again. We threaded our way through the beginning of the rush hour and on to the motorway. Sheila said nothing, knowing how hard I have to concentrate to drive a car.

At Scratchwood Services I pulled in, hoping the sleet would stop while we had a tea-break. The café was crowded with half the population of the North and the Midlands who'd had the same idea.

As we found places and cleared a space on a table Sheila looked around her. 'Do you know,' she said, wonderingly, 'right up to the time I left people who I like and respect, students and colleagues and friends with good brains, were saying how much they envied me, because I was flying off for a year in England. I was going to have the chance to really see the Old Country.' She shook her head. 'So far, it's snowed and I've been to a snag-and-chips café, spent the afternoon in a Victorian prison and here I am, dining with the man of my dreams in a motorway services.'

'It's not snow,' I said, 'we call it sleet when it's mixed with rain.'

'Yeah? The Eskimos have a lot of words for it too. We only have one, because we don't have snow in South Australia.'

'You may not know it,' I said, 'but this is a historic spot in its own right.'

She looked around again with an expression of utter disbelief. 'Oh, really?' she said flatly.

'You might not believe it,' I said, 'but this was once a huge rubbish dump, famous as the spot where two tramps

– known as Moosh and Tiggy – who lived in the dump murdered a mate of theirs and buried him in the rubbish.'

'Fascinating,' she said, even more flatly.

I raised both hands. 'All right! All right! I admit that it's been a bit of an odd day and not the brightest welcome back to Britain but you did come at me rather sudden and I have to fit things in where I can,' and regretted the last phrase as soon as I said it.

'OK, Tyroll, apology accepted. What are you going to do to make it up to me?' and she rubbed a leg against mine under the table.

'Er, how about a traditional English Victorian Christmas with all the trimmings?'

'Oh, you mean starving beggars and kids up chimneys and girls down coal mines and all that?'

'Well, no, actually. We don't have many coal mines left and the chimneys have given way to central heating. We still have the starving beggars, though. Actually I was thinking of turkey and stuffing and brandy and that.'

She grinned. 'Some of it sounds good, anyway.' She swigged her coffee. 'What about this Walton character, then? You were pretty tough on him, weren't you?'

'I told him, he's in a tough game and he's not likely to win.'

'Is he really innocent, do you think?'

'I haven't the faintest idea.'

She gave me a peculiar look. 'Doesn't it matter?' she said.

'Not to me it doesn't – it can't. It's the court's job to decide guilt or innocence, not mine or the cops'.'

'But don't you think about it?'

'Of course I do. But I don't know enough about Walton's case and there are a number of peculiarities about it.'

'So he's got a lawyer who doesn't care whether he's innocent and thinks he's got Buckley's.'

'Buckley's?'

'It's Aussie for a slim chance – as in "You've got two chances, mate, Buckley's and none." '

'What chance did Buckley take?'

'I don't remember – jumped his horse off an impossible cliff, or something.'

'Well, that's right. That's about Alan Walton's chance with the Court of Appeal, and anyway, I'm not his lawyer. I'm his mother-in-law's lawyer. If I'm lucky he'll get Legal Aid and a barrister will be assigned to present his case and I won't have to think about it again.'

'You really don't want to do it?'

'I really don't want to do it.'

'Why not?'

'Because it's old and difficult and peculiar and because Saffary's in it which will distort my judgements, and because I may get to believe Alan Walton is innocent and I won't be able to get him out. Are those enough reasons?'

'And when it goes wrong, little Granny Cassidy will smile at you and twinkle those bright, black eyes, and you'll do it, won't you?'

'Stop trying to cheer me up. Let's go.'

We crept back to Belston along the sleet-shrouded motorway and at last I pulled gratefully to a halt outside my home in Whiteway Village. I saw the porch light and the sitting-room light on and knew that Mrs Dunk, my cleaner, had carried out her instructions.

We lumbered Sheila's luggage into the hall, shucked off some outer layers and went into the sitting-room. Mrs Dunk had done me proud. A well-established fire burned in the grate and on a side table by the settee were an inviting bottle and a covered tray of snacks.

'Welcome,' I said, 'to the essential of an English Christmas – an open fire.'

'Beauty!' Sheila said. 'But shouldn't there be nuts roasting on it?'

'Complain, complain, complain! You've been listening to too many American songs.'

I pulled her down on to the settee with me and stifled her response. It was quite a long time before she shook herself free and reached for the wine.

Later, when she had turned out the lamps, she sprawled on the rug in front of the fire with a glass of wine. 'Come down here,' she invited.

'I've had a long hard day,' I said.

'So have I,' she said. 'How about finishing with a long, hard evening? There's nothing on the telly.'

'The last time you lured me with that excuse somebody fire-bombed us,' I said.

'Trust me – I'm a doctor!'

'Yeah – of history!'

'So nothing I do can kill you.'

With that guarantee I slid down to her side.

'Besides,' she said, 'I want to know what roasted nuts are like.'

6

From that point on, Christmas got better and better. On the last working day the office closed at lunch-time. Out came Jayne's Birthdays Bottle and her Accidents and Emergencies Bottle and several others as well. With a couple of Mary's robust cakes we all sprawled around the general office, while friends and colleagues dropped in to bring us a drink or to scrounge one or several.

Macintyre the pathologist came, bringing a bottle of Talisker, kissing the secretaries and sending them into shrieks with his seasonal tales of death and disembowelment. Claude the Phantom, our friendly neighbourhood private eye, joined us, bringing a huge bag of mince pies. Acting Detective Inspector Parry arrived. The stuffed kangaroo, a popular gift with the staff, squatted on top of a filing cabinet, a paper hat askew over one ear and a bottle of Oxford Landing in its pouch.

I squatted in a corner with Sheila and looked around me.

'What about Christmas in England so far?' I asked her.

She toasted me with her glass. 'Bonzer!' she said. 'You've got some good mates here, Chris Tyroll.'

I clinked glasses. 'Too right!' I said.

A bit later Macintyre was in full flood, reminiscing about some drunken hospital porters on duty at Christmas who, rather than manhandle a corpse down four flights of stairs, dropped it out of a window into a snowdrift and then couldn't find it. I went into my own office to dig out my reserve cigarettes. John Parry followed me.

'Got some news for you,' he said.

'Give me the bad first,' I said. 'The headlines are always bad at Christmas.'

'Saffary's back,' he said. 'Is that bad enough for you?'

I nodded. 'Pretty bad,' I said, 'but I thought it would happen.'

'What did HQ say about your complaint?'

'Oh, they sent me a load of carefully written gobbledegook, to the effect that, while I had undoubtedly been the victim of a complex and serious crime, and while they had to admit that the evidence indicated the involvement of an officer or officers of the Central Midlands Police, they regretted that it was not possible to identify the culprits, so no disciplinary or criminal proceedings would be brought against anyone. Yours faithfully, Chief Superintendent Scribble, for Chief Constable.'

It was the big Welshman's turn to nod.

'Where does it leave you? Saffary being back?' John had been made Acting Inspector when I succeeded in getting Saffary kicked sideways, six months before.

'That's the good news. As from January first my

promotion is confirmed.' He flashed his lapels and grinned broadly.

'Congratulations,' I said, and I meant it. 'Let's go back and have a drink on it.'

He put out a restraining hand. 'Hold on, boyo. Saffary's after you already, Chris. He was in the Police Club last night, sneering about the Belstone Lane case being appealed again. He said you'd been to the Scrubs to see one of them.'

'It's nothing,' I said. 'Alan Walton is Granny Cassidy's son-in-law. She asked me to see him. I'm not acting for him and I don't think much of his chances.'

'Just watch yourself, that's all.'

'Right,' I said and we went back to the party, where the announcement of John's promotion used up the last of the booze. I was filled with the seasonal spirit of goodwill, and if it didn't extend to Saffary I wasn't going to see him as a threat.

The Christmas holiday with Sheila in my home was like all the best Christmases of childhood rolled into one and for several days I forgot Granny Cassidy, Alan Walton and Inspector Saffary. When we got back to work I wrote to her as kind a letter as I could construct, setting out my realistic appraisal of Alan's chances.

On New Year's Eve she rang me at the office, to tell me that Alan and his mate had been granted Legal Aid and leave to present their application to the Court of Appeal. I asked her to pass on my congratulations and drew a silent breath of relief.

'There's just one thing you could do for me, Mr Tyroll, if you will,' she said.

'What's that?' I asked.

'I'm too old and slow to go to London when the appeal is on. Will you go for me?'

On the phone I couldn't even see her little black eyes but I said yes anyway. It seemed harmless at the time. I was too puddled by love and Christmas to see that the Belstone Lane case was beginning to slide down on top of me.

7

The Court of Appeal sits in London at the Royal Courts of Justice in the Strand, a strange Gothic building reminiscent of vampires. I refused to drive down again so Sheila and I went by train.

Beyond the inevitable security screen at the entrance to the Royal Courts is a breathtaking Gothic hall, which duly impressed the tourist in Sheila, not to mention a display of historic robes which impressed the historian in her. The case was listed to be heard in the afternoon so we made for the restaurant.

Sheila looked at the sandwich packet she was opening. 'I don't believe it!' she laughed. 'Royal bloody sandwiches!' and she pointed to the crown printed on the wrapper.

'We are', I said solemnly, 'in Her Majesty's Royal Courts of Justice and that was Her sandwich.'

'I can just imagine her getting up early to cut it,' she said. 'It's not a raw prawn sandwich, you know.'

'There used to be a tramp who bought sandwiches in here and then sold them to tourists on the streets. He used to tell them they were left-overs from Buckingham Palace. Had a good trade, I believe.'

She laughed loudly, a sound not often heard in those precincts. 'You mean somewhere in Tokyo or Sioux Falls there are framed wrappers like this one? Marvellous!'

As we left the table she asked, 'You still reckon he's got Buckley's?'

'Yes,' I said.

We made our way through the low, Gothic arches that

lead back into the main hall, and took a staircase. On landings above the hall are the courtrooms. As we pushed through two sets of glass doors, Sheila looked round at the panelled room, lit by high windows.

'Don't you have any modern courts?' she asked.

'Sure. There's a new building at the back of this one – all chilly air-conditioning in the courts and stuffy waiting areas, but they use that mainly for civil hearings. When it comes to the liberty of the subject and being told that you've got to go on doing your time, we believe in the full Victorian panoply.'

'Oh well,' she said, 'I wanted Dickens . . .'

'Dickens was long dead before we had a Court of Appeal,' I said. 'It may look like pure Victorian, but actually it was invented early in this century. There were a few obviously wrong convictions and Parliament got fed up with passing special Acts to undo them, so it set up the Court of Appeal.'

We sat in the raised public benches at the rear. A few places had been taken by the curious and those who had come in out of the cold, and an elderly couple a few feet away looked as if they might be Grady's parents. We had not been seated long when three robed and wigged judges shuffled on to the high bench above the court and the lawyers rose and bowed to them.

Sheila was looking around. 'Where's Walton?' she whispered.

I looked around. 'If he was here, he'd be up there,' I said and pointed to a little panelled box, high up on the right. 'It's a bad sign.'

'What is?'

'That he's not been brought from the Scrubs. That, and listing it in the afternoon. It means they're not expecting to waste much time on it and they don't want him here to see them chuck his application out.'

She shook her head. 'You'd think they'd let him come. Who is everybody?'

'The three old blokes in robes and fancy wigs are the judges. The blokes in black gowns and wigs down there are the barristers and the people sitting immediately behind them are solicitors and clerks. Keep quiet – Grady's barrister is about to kick off.'

A young man, whose clean white wig betrayed his lack of years in practice, had risen. He began to outline the argument I had read in Walton's application – that the officers who investigated the case had now been disciplined for serious offences in another robbery case and that, as a result, Grady's assertions at the trial that his confession statement had been faked were now more believable. Had the jury at Stafford, he argued, known of the officers' behaviour in the other case, they would have been less likely to convict. The convictions were unsafe and unsatisfactory and his client should be granted leave to present an appeal to the court.

He concluded in a few minutes, bobbed his head to the judges and sat. Walton's barrister rose alongside him, an older man with a greyer, scruffier wig. The judges were talking among themselves.

Eventually the presiding judge turned back to the court. 'Thank you, Mr Wegg,' he said to Grady's barrister. 'Before you address us on behalf of the applicant Walton, Mr Grocutt,' he went on, 'there is a preliminary point which we should like to clarify, one that may save a deal of time.'

He cleared his throat. 'It seems to us that the first hurdle, as it were, in this application, is the believability of the statement which, it is alleged by the Crown, was given freely and voluntarily by the applicant Grady. If we accept that the disciplinary proceedings subsequently taken against officers in the case cast doubt on the truth of that document, if, as Mr Wegg would have us believe, that statement was not voluntarily given, but was extracted by force or fraud or if it is in itself faked in some way, then it is obvious that this court must consider whether the jury at

Stafford would have felt able to convict had it known of that situation.

'In the case of both applicants there is, of course, a second hurdle – the evidence of the witness Mrs Simpson, but it may be that we can leave that issue in abeyance for the present at least. Mr Grocutt, may we take it that you agree with the proposition that both of these applications depend, in the first place, on the question of the credibility of Grady's confession statement – that that question is as much at the heart of your client's case as that of his fellow applicant?'

Grocutt bobbed his head and murmured his agreement. It was self-evidently right. He didn't see the trap, Wegg didn't see the trap and certainly I didn't.

'Then,' the judge continued, 'I believe that we can shorten these proceedings.'

I had expected little of this hearing, but now I began to suspect that the court had something new up its sleeve. It did.

'Apprised', said the judge, 'of the nature of this application, we thought it right to institute certain enquiries. The single judge in giving leave for this application to come before us was aware, as any newspaper reader is aware and as was recited in both of the applications, that investigations into the conduct of certain officers of the Central Midlands Police had resulted in disciplinary action against the late Detective Chief Inspector Hawkins and Inspector Watters in another case. He was quite right to permit this matter to be aired here. Taking the view which I have already put, that the credibility of the Grady confession is crucial to both applications, a proposition which both counsel have accepted, we have caused an enquiry to be made with the Chief Constable of the Central Midlands as to the precise nature of the proceedings against those officers. I am sure that applicants' counsel will equally agree that this information is essential to any decision on the applications.'

He paused to allow counsel to agree with him. Both nodded dumbly. They were beginning to catch on.

'I have here', he said, 'a letter written on behalf of the Chief Constable in answer to the query which we directed to him. It is dated 29th December last year and reads as follows:

'"I have been asked by the Chief Constable to reply to your enquiry of 20th December in respect of disciplinary proceedings taken against Detective Chief Inspector Hawkins and Inspector Watters of this force.

'"From records before me I can confirm that, on 15th July 1998, both of these officers appeared before a disciplinary hearing as a result of enquiries into their conduct in the case of R. v. Altaf Hussain. They were both charged identically, namely that 'In pursuing enquiries in the case of Altaf Hussain they failed to observe proper procedures or to maintain proper records of their enquiries'.

'"It will, perhaps, assist you if I point out that although both officers were found to be guilty of this charge, the charge related only to the keeping of proper records and documentation. It was in no way concerned with the conduct of any interview, whether with a witness or suspect, nor was it alleged that any suspect had been improperly treated by the officers.

'"You may not be aware that Detective Chief Inspector Hawkins is now deceased."

'That letter is signed by Chief Superintendent Lawson on behalf of his Chief Constable.'

In the silence that followed the reading, counsel for the prosecution rose for the first time.

'My Lords,' he began, 'it seems to me that, in the light of the chief superintendent's information – '

He got no further before the judge interrupted him. 'Yes, Mr Randle, in the light of that letter it appears that both of the applications now before us are based upon a false premise – namely, that officers in the case are now known to have misbehaved in their treatment of a suspect in the Hussain case. Since we are now aware that no such proposition can be supported it is the view of this court that these applications must fail. Our detailed reasons will be issued in due course.'

He pulled his robe around him and rose, shuffling off the bench with his two colleagues.

'The bastards!' I breathed. I knew now that the Belstone Lane case had just become virtually impossible and that it had finally fallen on my head.

8

Tourists love the Temple – the Victorian rookery where London's barristers roost. A network of crooked lanes, emerald lawns and handsome old buildings, peopled by bewigged and gowned barristers and lit by ancient gas-lamps, it stands a few yards from the Law Courts.

The price of Sheila's company in the Court of Appeal had been the promise of a visit to the Temple, and now she strolled its lanes with wide eyes and a busy camera, exclaiming as a genuine lamplighter ambled past us in the winter twilight and went about his duties in front of her lens. I followed blindly behind her, immune for once to the Temple's charm, turning over the Belstone Lane case.

Eighteen years ago four unknown men had ambushed a security van. A guard had been killed and another maimed. Despite an enormous manhunt, no charges were brought for six years. Then Glenys Simpson had named her husband and three friends as the robbers. The police had arrested three men not including Billy Simpson. Simpson had committed suicide. Grady had signed a confession statement, whether genuine or not. He had been charged. Walton had denied any knowledge of the robbery. He had been charged. Freddy Hughes had denied all knowledge of the robbery. He had not been charged. Walton and Grady had been convicted on a combination of Grady's 'confession' and Glenys Simpson's evidence. Hawkins and Watters, the interviewing officers in the case, had been disciplined. Walton and Grady had revived their appeals and got as far as a hearing before the full court.

It didn't make much sense, but it got worse. So far from Walton and Grady's appeals failing on the evidence of Glenys Simpson, the court had produced its hidden ace and thrown the appeals out on the statement of the police that Hawkins and Watters were done for only administrative offences – and that, I was sure, was simply not true. The Central Midlands police, over the signature of a chief superintendent acting for the Chief Constable, had lied to the Court of Appeal to make doubly sure that Walton and Grady did their twenty years.

On the train back to Brum I continued my silence. Sheila was equally silent, plying me with coffees from the buffet and reading a magazine until we were half-way home. Then she put down her reading, sipped her coffee and leaned across the table to me.

'OK, Chris Tyroll, are you going to talk about it or not?'

I looked up and said nothing.

'Come on!' she said. 'Ever since the decision you've been moping about like a one-legged bloke at an arse-kicking contest.'

I grinned, in spite of my mood. 'OK, get me something stronger from the bar and I'll talk.'

She came back with a couple of whiskies and I set out my argument. She nodded when I had finished.

'But you always expected the case to be thrown out.'

'Yes, but I thought they'd do it in two stages. I thought they'd accept that there was doubt over Grady's statement then say, "But Glenys Simpson's evidence stands unchallenged and the jury could have convicted on that so no cigar." '

'So they threw it out for a different reason. What's the difference?'

'Look – the investigation into the Central Midlands police has given them a hell of a bad press. A number of big cases have gone belly up. In the remote eventuality that the Court of Appeal had let this one through, it couldn't have done the police much more harm. What's more, they must have seen it the way I did – that it might succeed on the first point, but it would fail on what their Lordships called the "second hurdle". So, all in all, they hadn't got much to worry about, right?'

She nodded and I went on. 'But something about this case is so important that the police wouldn't rely on the court to give them a way out, they had to give it a shove in the right direction – a bloody big shove!'

'The letter?'

'Exactly. That letter is nothing more than a bare-faced lie.'

'How do you know?'

'I'll show you when we get home.'

Back at the ranch, Sheila's appetite led her straight to the kitchen. I picked up the phone and relayed the bad news to Granny Cassidy. She was very philosophical about it, thanked me for going to London, then she asked, 'He don't get any more Legal Aid now, do he?'

'No,' I said.

'So he don't have to have a lawyer from the court?'

'No.'

'Do it for him, Mr Tyroll. Do it for him and our Tracy. She'm breaking her heart for him. It's been twelve years, Mr Tyroll. Will you do it?'

By the time Sheila called me to the table I was scrabbling glumly through the magazine rack by my armchair.

'What you after?' she enquired.

'This,' I announced, triumphantly brandishing a magazine. I took it to the table with me.

'I hope', she said, 'you're not going to turn out to be one of those blokes who reads at the table.'

'Just this once,' I said and turned to the article I had been seeking. I found the passage I wanted and passed it across to her. 'Read that!'

Fork in one hand, magazine in the other, she read the paragraph I had indicated.

'"ESDA tests on Hussain's so-called confession statement revealed that the pages had been written out of sequence. As a result, the Court of Appeal quashed Hussain's robbery conviction and Hawkins and Watters were brought before a disciplinary hearing." '

She laid the paper down. 'What's ESDA?' she asked.

'Electronic Static Deposition Analysis – it's a technique for discovering pressure marks on documents where another sheet of paper has lain over it and something else has been written on the top sheet. ESDA brings up the image of the pressure marks so that it can be photographed.'

'You mean like kids' secret writing when you write the message on the top sheet and send the blank underneath sheet. The person who gets it just has to rub it with cigarette ash and the outline of the letters comes up?'

'Very much the same, only being expensive and important scientists they do it with complicated machines to create an electro-static field around the paper and use iron-filings instead of cigarette ash.'

'So Hawkins and Watters were done for tampering with interview evidence?'

'Right – and the police lied about it and the court pretended that the press had never reported exactly what Watters and Hawkins had done. There's got to be something very dirty about the case for the force to have lobbed that letter into court.'

Over coffee she asked, 'What do you think about Walton's innocence now?'

'If it's any satisfaction to you, I now think he may well be innocent, but it doesn't help.'

'Why not?'

'Because he's served twelve years and it looks like he's going to have to do the other eight – innocent or not.'

9

Despite Sheila's presence beside me, I slept badly that night. Vanloads of masked judges and policemen swept through my nightmares, brandishing shotguns. At some point in the night I must have woken and extracted something rational from my fantasies, for when I woke in the morning I found I had scribbled a note on my bedside pad:

The Payday Gang?
Freddy Hughes?
Glenys Simpson?
When/How did Hawkins die?
Ring magazine.

Sheila had her own business that day. She had extracted some information from the Public Records Office on convicts transported from the Midlands, and now she was delving into local records to see if she could trace their families.

'I'll bet', I suggested, 'that when you turn up on some self-made double-glazing millionaire's doorstep in Little Aston, he's going to be really delighted to learn that his great-great-great-great-grandfather was transported for sheep-shagging!'

'They didn't,' she said. 'They hanged you for that. You only got transported for stealing them.'

'Ah,' I said, sadly, 'the Permissive Society has a lot to answer for.'

I had a dull morning in Belston Magistrates' Court filled with four guilty pleas in a row, the hopeless kind where what you really ought to tell the court is that anyone who repeated the same offence as often as your client, did it so badly and got caught so often, deserved the court's sympathy and a cosy place in a funny farm.

Late morning found me in a back booth of the Rendezvous Café, across the square from the court, polishing off a buttered Chelsea bun with a mug of Ruby's orange tea, and musing idly over my bedside note. John Parry found me there and joined me with more Chelseas and his own mug.

'Whatever happened to the Payday Gang, John?' I asked him.

'Ah!' he exclaimed. 'Nostalgia trivia – I love that! What was Adam Ant's first hit? What was Tiny Tim's only hit? Who was the first Minister for Sport?'

'Seriously,' I insisted. 'What happened to them?'

He swallowed a gulp of tea. 'The duly authorised forces of law and order tracked them to their lair, took them into custody and they were all locked up.'

'Really? When was that?'

'Oh, round about Royal Wedding, urban riots time – early eighties. '81 or '82.'

'What happened?'

'The Regional Crime Squad had them. About twenty of them went up at Birmingham Crown Court. Huge indictment – umpteen robberies and attempts. So far as I know, all of them went down for years and years.'

'How would I find out more about it?'

'Local papers, I suppose. *Express and Star, Evening Mail, Birmingham Post* files. The trial had a lot of coverage.'

He looked at me over his tea. 'This got anything to do with your trip to London?'

'Good grief!' I said. 'Can't a bloke take his girlfriend to London without your lot taking an interest?'

He tapped his broad nose with a forefinger. 'Not a sparrow falls, boyo, and don't give me that innocent trip to London bit. You were in the Court of Appeal. Not many tourists in there – particularly not in January.'

'All right, guv. It's a fair cop! I was asked to go and watch an application on behalf of an interested party.'

He nodded. 'The Belstone Lane case. Went down, didn't it?'

'What's your interest?' I asked.

He looked exaggeratedly innocent. 'Mine? None at all, except keeping you around and in business to buy me buttered Chelseas and pursue your vendetta against Saffary till you bounce him and open my road to the Chief Constable's desk.'

'Who says I've got a vendetta against Saffary?'

'Well, he does, for one. And you'd better have, 'cos he's certainly got one against you. He's always hated you.'

'Why?'

'Obvious, innit, boyo? You're a lawyer who defends people, you're some kind of leftie or anarchist or whatnot and you look as if you might be foreign. Any one of them would be enough for Saffary, but it's worse than that. Ever since he made Sergeant he'd had a perfect record to hear him talk, commendations and all, until you put the boot in last summer. Got a brooding, vengeful, sort of personality, he has. Says he's a Christian, but he seems to forget the bit about forgiving your enemies.'

'He said so?'

'Yes. He and a tableful of his cronies were making life hideous in the Police Club last night. They were celebrating the appeal going down.'

He swallowed tea again. 'I hate that. Police officers have

no legitimate interest in the outcome of a case. It's our job to put suspects in front of the courts. After that it's up to the courts.'

'What did he say about me?'

'I asked what they were celebrating and he told me. Then he said, "Your pal Tyroll was at the hearing with his Australian bit. Next time you see him, tell him to keep his nose out of the Belstone Lane case." So, here I am, delivering his message.'

'There's something very rotten about the Belstone Lane thing, John,' I said.

'What a surprise, bach! With Hawkins, Watters and Saffary in it I'd be bloody surprised if there wasn't!'

Mention of Hawkins reminded me of my notes. 'What happened to Hawkins?' I asked.

'Detective Chief Inspector Hawkins', he said, 'took early retirement on grounds of ill-health after his name had been splashed all over the tabloids.'

'What ill-health? I remember him as a big, well-set-up looking bloke. Always wore handmade suits and smoked little cigars. Didn't look as if he'd ever had a day's illness in his life.'

'That's the man. All sharp suits, yellow-tinted specs and monograms on his silk shirts. Dropped dead, he did, just after retiring. They found him dead in his garden. Heart attack, they said.'

He shook his head. 'It really surprised some of us. We never knew the bastard had a heart.'

'Anything suspicious about it?' I asked.

'Come on, now!' he said. 'Just because you and Sheila found me a murder last summer doesn't mean you've got a nose for 'em. Hawkins dropped dead in his garden. End of story. Anyway – who'd kill him?'

'It was two murders last summer,' I said, 'and just because you're a police officer doesn't mean you've got a properly suspicious mind. Anyone might have killed him. Half the wrongful convictions in the Midlands must have been down to him and anyway he could have been killed by a partner in crime – he must have had plenty of them.'

'His regular cronies used to be Watters and Saffary. D'you reckon one of them had him with that untraceable poison that we never come across except in novels? I'd have you know that us guardians of law and order only kill each other for promotion.'

'I take it', I said, 'that you weren't involved in the Belstone Lane case at all?'

'Not me, boyo,' he said, with a mouth full of Chelsea, 'I was otherwise engaged at the time. In fact, I thought it was a Payday Gang job till now.'

'Could it have been?'

'Apart from the shooting, yes – but the shooting's always accidental in these things, anyway. You go tooled up long enough and sooner or later a gun's going to go off, innit?'

He finished his Chelsea bun and looked surprised that it was the last. 'It occurs to me,' he said, 'that you already have a contact with someone who knows about the Payday Gang.'

'Who's that?' I said.

'Malcolm Raikes – didn't you use to defend him?'

'Yes,' I said, slowly. 'I got him off three times – but he was never anything to do with the Payday Gang.'

'While we were trying to put Raikes away for receiving stolen gear,' he said, 'the Regional Crime Squad thought he was a planner for the Payday Gang. It just so happened that we got him first, he dropped you as his brief – '

'That's right!' I interrupted. 'And paid the price of his folly by getting five years for receiving. What's he doing now?'

'Doesn't seem to have learned his lesson – he's an antiques dealer, importing and exporting.'

10

You might have thought that Malcolm Raikes was pure public school – that's if you hadn't seen him through three acquittals in the Crown Court and read the probation and antecedent reports. In fact he was pure Walsall, out of a council house in Harden. In his youth he took to the local trade – stealing – and wasn't very good at it. He graduated via the juvenile courts to a spell in Borstal and on to Winson Green. A short stay there seemed to convince him that he was misapplying his talents. Suddenly he stopped.

It was not, of course, because he was going straight, merely because he'd had the wit to withdraw to a less exposed area of the profession – receiving. No police officer for miles believed he was straight and they continued to arrest him, but they didn't get convictions. I'd like to think that his immunity was down to my forensic skills but it rested entirely on Raikes' fertile and creative imagination.

He would call me to say that he'd been arrested and charged. Since the charge was always some form of dishonesty, he always had the right of trial in the Crown Court. 'Put it up for trial by jury,' he'd drawl, 'and I'll tell you about it when you've got the prosecution evidence.'

So the case would be adjourned for committal to the Crown Court, the Crown Prosecution Service would supply me with copies of their witness statements and I would have a meeting with Malcolm and read over them. He would listen, gravely, and without breaking sweat or batting an eyelid would answer each point in the Crown evidence so reasonably that it was hard to imagine why he'd ever been suspected.

When he'd done there would be a complete and reasonable answer to the prosecution case – and he did it all in his head as I read over the statements. If there were slight rough patches in his account those would be smoothed over by Crown witnesses suddenly losing their memory in the witness box or even failing to show up. That was how he got acquitted.

Then he got pulled for receiving the proceeds of a robbery in Shropshire. For reasons I never understood, he took his business elsewhere and his creative powers must have failed him. Two old ladies had been badly roughhoused in the robbery and he went down for five years.

His last address known to me was a farm, a few miles out of Cannock. I rang him and told him that I wanted to discuss something better kept off the phone. He was used to that approach and invited me over.

The cab dropped me in a secondary road, alongside a painted wooden sign that said 'Melford House'. I had wanted to get a look at the house and it was worth it. It stood behind the trees that screened it from the road, a perfect medium-sized eighteenth-century manor. If it was bought on the proceeds of antiques dealing, he must have been specialising in Crown Jewels.

Malcolm was waiting for me at the door, supporting his image with cavalry twill slacks, a cream linen shirt (with obligatory monogram on pocket), and paisley cravat. With his deep tan and carefully cut grey hair he looked as distinguished as he intended.

'Mr Tyroll!' he exclaimed. 'What a pleasure to see you again! Do come in.'

He led me through a large hall, hung with paintings of which I only caught a glimpse, and into a study that looked out over a wide lawn to Cannock Chase.

I looked around me as he poured me a whisky. The room was lined with bookshelves. They say you can tell a lot about a man from his books. All I could tell about Raikes was that he had bought his books by the yard. They were all beautifully bound Victorian editions of standard works of literature and I don't imagine he'd ever opened one of them. On the corner of his desk stood a pile of his real reading – antiques guides, telephone directories and airline timetables.

'You've done well,' I said.

'Well,' he said, 'after that last unfortunate affair I decided to move upmarket. It was buying from the wrong people that got me into trouble, you know. Now I have no doubts where the goods come from because I only deal with the best. In fact, I'm just helping to furnish a house for . . .' and he mentioned a minor Royal.

'That was the beginning of my good fortune,' he went on. 'I'd just walked out of Winson Green when I got a message that he wanted my help. Well, I couldn't go and see him fresh out of prison and looking like it, so I sent him a note from my non-existent secretary saying that Mr Raikes had been abroad for a while but would rush back to deal with his enquiry. Then I shot off to Spain and lay on a beach for days until I was brown enough to look as if I'd been in Australia.'

I chuckled and he sipped his drink. 'It was very well worth it,' he said. 'That introduction made me what I am today. But enough about me. You were very mysterious on the phone. What can I do for you?'

It suddenly occurred to me that this was embarrassing. To sit in a bloke's posh study, drink his whisky and then ask him if he wasn't the brains behind a bunch of armed robbers – let alone going on to ask if they hadn't committed murder. I decided to approach obliquely.

'Do you know a man called Alan Walton?' I asked.

He seemed genuinely puzzled. 'I don't think so. What does he do?'

'At the moment he's doing twenty in the Scrubs.'

He winced. 'That must have been for something pretty bad.'

'It was. Armed robbery in which one man died and another man was crippled.'

His eyes narrowed. 'The Belstone Lane robbery,' he said. 'What on earth makes you think I know anything about that, Mr Tyroll?'

'You'll remember that there was an armed gang around at the time, known as the Payday Gang.'

His eyes narrowed further. 'Ye-es,' he said, slowly.

'The Payday Gang, or most of them, were rounded up by the Regional Crime Squad and weighed off at Birmingham.'

'Yes.'

'Well, a little bird tells me – a very authoritative little bird – that back in the bad old days you had a connection with the Payday Gang.'

He smiled slowly. 'The police always thought so,' he said. 'They had a race – Regional Crime Squad versus the County CID – to see who could nail me first. What's your interest in the Payday Gang?'

'Alan Walton,' I said, 'is my client. He's one of two men serving twenty years for the Belstone Lane job. He says he didn't do it.'

'Don't they all say that?'

'Well, you said it to me three times,' I said.

He smiled again. '*Touché*. And you believe him?'

'Normally it's not my job to believe or disbelieve, but in this case I've got a good reason for believing that there's something wrong.'

He nodded. 'And if I did know anything about the Payday Gang, what would they have to do with it?'

'The Payday Gang had operated so long and so successfully in the Midlands that it seems unlikely to me that anyone else would have muscled in on their act. The Belstone Lane job was exactly like a Payday Gang job. It seems to me that they're the people who are most likely to have done it.'

'Imitation is the sincerest form of flattery,' he smiled.

'But suppose for a moment that it was the Payday Gang. If I had the kind of connection you mentioned, do you really think I'd give you the evidence to hang a murder rap on old colleagues? You're a lot smarter than that, Mr Tyroll.'

It was my turn to smile. 'So are you, Mr Raikes. That's not what I'm asking for. Let me put a few theoretical questions and let's see where it goes.'

He nodded.

'Do you think it could have been the Payday Gang?'

He nodded again.

'Is there anything you can tell me which will lead me in the right direction?' He thought for a moment then he nodded once more and pulled a notepad towards him. He scribbled on it and passed me the torn-off page.

'George Cook,' I read. 'He can help me?'

'If you can find him and if he will.'

'Where will I find him?'

'He hangs about your area, Belston and around. He's also known as Banjo Cook.'

'Because he banjoes people?'

He looked hurt. 'No, because he plays it.'

'Is there anything else you can tell me?'

He shook his head. I finished my drink and stood up. As he walked me to the door, I asked, 'What made you change solicitors? I'd played three and won three.'

'Embarrassment,' he said. 'I was so stupid over the Shropshire job that I knew they'd have me. I didn't want you to think I was an idiot.'

I laughed. 'Never!' I said.

'Don't you be an idiot either, Mr Tyroll,' he said at the door. 'There's some hard people about. Just remember I'm not the only antiques dealer in the world and I'm not the only one that the Royals deal with.'

He tapped his nose with a finger and closed the front door firmly behind me. As I walked back to the cab I felt embarrassed at suggesting that he consorted with killers. With hindsight, I suppose I shouldn't have done.

11

To be strictly accurate we ought to call him Lon or Erik, but we've called him Claude the Phantom for years. It started back in the old days when enquiry agents made a lot of their living in matrimonial work – following suspected spouses about. Claude had a bumper season with an adulterous couple who were into opera. Night after night he sat in the stalls of every amateur operatic society from Coventry to Stoke on Trent. Claude's real name is Gordon Rains and some office wit recalled that Claude Raines had played the Phantom of the Opera. It was only after the nickname had stuck that anyone remembered that Lon Chaney played the part first and anyway the Phantom's real name was Erik.

I asked him to find Banjo Cook for me. Not much to go on – just a name and a nickname and the fact that he usually hung around Belston – but I knew that if anyone could find Cook, Claude could.

I was right. Two days later Claude reported that he'd tracked Cook to a boarding house on the Wolverhampton road, a place called 'Bert's Café' though it hadn't been a café for years. I hadn't asked Claude to interview Cook, largely because I didn't know what to ask him and I wanted to do it myself and play it by ear.

I guessed that the best time to catch Cook might be early evening – before he settled into a pub somewhere. When the office closed one afternoon Sheila and I went along there.

It was a pretty sad place. The downstairs front had been Bert's Café, then a sex shop and lastly a junk shop. Its plate glass was cracked and dusty and partly boarded up. To the right of the old shop entrance was a private door, over which a sixty watt bulb glimmered through a dusty fanlight.

I tried the private door and it opened, letting us into a narrow, dirty hallway with a payphone on one wall. Thirty feet back the hallway gave on to a wide, dark room lit only by a flickering television set. When my eyes had adjusted to the gloom I could see that there were battered couches and armchairs round the walls. Huddled on one of them was a little old man with lank grey hair.

'We're looking for George Cook,' I said.

His gaze remained fastened on the television. I repeated my remark, louder.

Still without turning his head he said, 'Cook? Banjo Cooky? Top flat, mate. Through there and up the stairs.'

He pointed into the gloom behind the TV and I could see another door. I thanked him and we followed his indication. Behind the door was a stairwell with uncarpeted stairs climbing away into the darkness. After a search we located a light switch that worked and, four flights up, we came to a dead end on a landing outside what had to be the top flat.

Knocking produced no response, so I tried the door. It opened and Sheila followed me into Cook's flat. The light was on and the room we had entered – apparently his sitting-room – was stiflingly hot from a paraffin heater turned high.

The light and the heater made me hope that Cook was in residence. I called his name. As I did so the door slammed behind us and a voice hissed, 'Keep quiet and don't move – either of you!'

We spun around. A man crouched with his back to the closed door. He was a stocky, fresh-complexioned man with close-cropped hair and a hard face.

'Are you George Cook?' I asked.

He laughed, shortly. 'No, I fucking ain't,' he said.

'Do you know where he is?' I asked. Everything about the man was threatening but I was trying not to escalate the situation.

He laughed again, the same ugly little bark. 'Oh yes,' he said. 'I know where Georgy is, but it don't matter to you.'

He slid his right hand into his leather jacket and a knife appeared in his hand. He swung it in front of him.

'Now,' he said, 'what's your business with Cooky?'

'None of yours,' retorted Sheila.

He took a pace towards her. 'Shut your mouth, bitch!' he snarled. 'I was asking yer boyfriend.'

'Don't call me a bitch, you snotty Pommy scumbag!' she said.

He lunged at her with his fist, keeping me back with the knife in his other hand. As soon as he moved, Sheila moved quicker. Her booted foot came up hard, taking him right in the crotch.

He howled and collapsed backwards. The knife skittered across the lino as he fell on to a couch, clutching his injury. I grabbed the weapon but Sheila swiftly took it from me and moved to stand in front of the man, who now huddled on the couch emitting a mixture of groans and obscenities.

'Find something to tie this bastard up, Chris,' she commanded. 'I'm going to whittle a few pieces off him while we find out who he is.' Her face looked as if she meant it – his looked as if he believed it.

I stepped through the door into a hallway. Three doors off it had to be the kitchen, bathroom and bedroom. Looking for the bedroom, where I might find ties or belts, I tried the first door. It was the bathroom.

I went back into the sitting-room. 'I've found a rope,' I said, 'but there's someone hanging on it – it must be Cook.'

It was just the distraction our guest needed. As Sheila glanced at me in surprise he scrambled over the arm of the couch and out of the door. We heard his footsteps clattering down the four flights of bare stairs.

I went back into the bathroom and Sheila followed. The body of a black man, about thirty-five, hung by a short cord from the shower fitment. I had touched his neck on first finding him. He was definitely dead.

We called the police from the payphone below and waited for them in Cook's sitting-room. Sheila's attack of bravado had vanished on seeing the body and we huddled on the couch smoking.

'You took a hell of a risk,' I said.

'Rubbish!' she said. 'As long as he was by the door with a knife, he'd got us cold. If we'd rushed him, one or both of us would have got hurt. If you'd challenged him he'd have ignored me and gone for you with the knife. It had to be me. He wasn't expecting trouble from a mere woman.'

'A mere woman!' I exclaimed. 'Where'd you learn to kick like that?'

'Australian Rules football,' she grinned.

'Come on,' I said. 'I know it's pretty rough, but that's not in the Australian Rules.'

'Well, no, but you do learn to kick hard and straight.'

Minutes later the police arrived and I was relieved to see that John Parry was with them, though I can't say he was particularly pleased to see us.

'I don't think', he said, 'that you understand the division of responsibilities properly. The police are supposed to detect murders and your lot are supposed to get the perpetrator acquitted in the face of the evidence. Anyway, what were you two doing in these unsalubrious surroundings?'

'I came to call on a possible witness,' I said.

'George Cook?' he asked. 'Well, he's witnessed a lot of things in his time. Which were you interested in?'

'Belstone Lane,' I said. 'Someone thought he might know about it.'

Parry whistled. 'Well now,' he said, 'you do surprise me!'

12

We were a long time making witness statements, after which Parry had us back at the police station ploughing through books of photographs to see if we could spot our attacker. We found him in the end, a man called Eddie Poxon with a long record of violence.

I reckoned that I owed Sheila – if only for saving my life for the second time in a few months – so we dined that evening at the Jubilee Room, the poshest that Belston has to offer. I was not the best company and eventually she complained.

'Come on, Chris,' she urged. 'You're mooning around like a – '

'Don't say it!' I interrupted. 'Not in here. I'll get barred for life and I'm not mooning around – I'm thinking.'

'What about?'

'That I had one lead in Walton's case. I didn't know what it meant, but I think it was a lead. That was Cook and now he's dead.'

'Who do you think killed him?' she asked. 'I mean, our friend with the knife presumably did, but why?'

'Well, the obvious answer is to stop him talking to me, but who the blazes knew I was looking for him?'

'Claude's been asking round for him for a couple of days, hasn't he?'

'But why would they think he was working for me? He does jobs for several firms.'

'Other way round,' she said. 'Someone knows you're in the Belstone case and is afraid you'll find Cook, so he keeps eyes and ears out for anyone looking for Cook and along comes Claude. It doesn't even have to be someone who knows about you, just someone who knows that there's fresh interest in the case.'

'Yes. I suppose that might have set somebody's alarm bells ringing – but whose?'

'The Payday Gang?' she suggested.

'What would be the point? If they did the Belstone Lane job and they're afraid of getting fingered for murder, killing Cook would just draw attention to the case. What if the police catch Poxon and he talks? They'd be worse off than they are now.'

'But if you were to succeed in getting Walton off . . .' she began, but I snorted.

She ignored me and carried on. '. . . wouldn't the police have to reinvestigate the case?'

I snorted again. 'When the Court of Appeal finally let the Birmingham Six out,' I said, 'the West Midlands police announced that they were going to reinvestigate the biggest mass murder in British history.'

'And . . . ?' she said.

'And a few weeks later coppers were joking about going round all the Irish pubs in Birmingham asking if anyone remembered a bloke called Paddy who used to drink there in 1974. If – and it's a bloody big if – Walton gets out, the police won't want to know. His appeal is no threat to the Payday Gang.'

'Who else, then?' she said.

'Well, so far the only people who we know are anxious to stop Walton are the police.'

'You're not seriously suggesting that Poxon was a police hit man?'

I grinned. 'Not really,' I said, 'but I ought to remind you that you once sat in this very room and told Mac and me that you didn't believe our theories about your grandfather's death.'

As if on cue, a Scots voice hailed us as Dr Macintyre

appeared beside the table. 'John Parry said you might be here,' he said.

'Pull up a chair,' I said. 'Join us for coffee, Mac.'

'I was hoping', he said, 'that there might be something a wee bit stronger.'

We removed to the lounge and ordered something stronger.

Macintyre smacked his lips after a hearty swallow of whisky. 'Aah!' he said. 'That takes away the smell of death.'

Sheila grinned. 'Tell me, Doc,' she said, 'do you only visit friends in restaurants when you're fresh from an autopsy?'

He shook his head. 'A post-mortem, lassie. The Yankees have autopsies – we have post-mortems, though I suppose it doesnae make a deal of difference from the customer's point of view.' He shook his head again and applied himself to his drink.

'Mac,' I said, 'do you think you could stop rambling and boozing long enough to tell us why you came?'

'Oh, aye, aye,' he said. 'I've just finished with yon fellow you found – Cook, wasn't it?'

'And what about him?'

'He was murdered.'

'Somehow I thought he might have been.'

He looked hurt. 'If you'll let me finish. He wasnae hangit till after he was dead.'

'So what did he die of?' asked Sheila.

'He had no marks of a fight – no contusions or abrasions – but he was killed by a single blow to the neck.'

'A karate chop?' I said.

'Aye, something of that sort. He must have been taken by surprise and killed with the one blow.'

Sheila frowned. 'And then he was strung up to make it look like hanging? Would that work?'

'It has been known,' he said. 'A fellow called Emmett Dunne killed his lover's husband with a chop to the throat, then hanged him up. The pathologist said it was suicide.'

'So how do we know it wasn't?' she asked.

'Because suspicion was aroused later and Professor Camps re-examined the remains. That reminds me, did I ever tell you about Francis Camps and the Spanish rape case?'

'No,' I said, 'and you're not going to. Sheila and I have had a long evening and I think it's time we turned in.'

'You shouldnae go messing with dead folks that don't concern you,' he grumbled, as though he owned every cadaver in town.

13

If I had any hope, it was that the police would pull in Poxon and he would talk, but it was a fairly slender hope. Nobody employs hit men who blab about who paid them. Poxon, however, disappeared from all his usual haunts leaving no forwarding address.

Something else turned up as well. Three large cartons of documents from Walton's former solicitor. On a snowy weekend I took them home, gritted my teeth and settled into reading them. Sheila's bundles from the Public Records Office were crowding me out of my study, so I stacked the boxes in the lounge and settled into an armchair by the fire.

Just under the lid were a couple of booklets of photographs in the royal blue card covers of the Central Midlands police. The first booklet contained shots of the vehicles in the lane taken from several angles. The second had pictures of the dead and injured men lying in their blood. Both of them bore exhibit numbers from the trial. The defence could not have argued that there had never been a robbery or that it wasn't in Belstone Lane or that nobody died or was injured, so most of the pictures were irrelevant, but crisp colour enlargements of blood and injury prejudice a jury wonderfully.

The essential bundle would be the statements made by prosecution witnesses and I dug that out and ploughed into it.

First was a statement by a witness who was never called at the trial. His evidence was accepted by both sides. He was a plan-drawer, who had produced a map of the Belstone Lane area.

Belstone Lane ran down his map in a series of shallow curves, making a T-junction at the bottom with the main road into Bellsich. Right of the junction was a roundabout which was the beginning of Bellsich High Street. Along the lane he had marked the homes of various witnesses.

Next was a statement by the Mantons security manager:

Name: Desmond Murphy
Age/DOB: 45. 14041935
Occupation: Security manager
Who states: This statement, consisting of 3 pages, each signed by me, is true to the best of my knowledge and belief and I make it knowing that if it is tendered in evidence I shall be liable to prosecution if I have wilfully stated in it anything which I know to be false or do not believe to be true.

After which he had dated and signed it before plunging into his narrative.

I am a former detective sergeant in the Central Midlands Police and I am now employed as Security Manager by Mantons Stores, based at their headquarters at Stoke on Trent. I am responsible for all the company's security arrangements in the Midland area, including the transit of cash.

The company operates a chain of general stores in several parts of the Midlands. Cash collections are made from these stores on Saturday evenings by a fleet of security vehicles operating from our headquarters.

Yesterday I assigned three vehicles to the Belston area which is the usual number. Each van has a crew of two, a driver and an assistant. All of the vans are white transits with no identifying name or logo on them.

Each van travels by a different route on each trip. I assign the routes and nobody else is aware of them until I give the collection sheets to the drivers when they leave headquarters.

Each van calls at a number of our shops. When each shop closes a manager or assistant manager waits for the security van to collect the takings. Using three vehicles allows us to call at each shop within a few minutes of the shop closing.

As well as several branches in Belston, we have two shops in Bellsich, and one van from Belston always travels to Bellsich to make the collections there before returning to headquarters. I always route that vehicle through Belstone Lane, rather than using the main road. I dislike having to use the same route but Belstone Lane is a quiet residential road, whereas the only alternative route from Belston to Bellsich is through a number of side streets which would, in my view, constitute a security risk.

From time to time I carry out spot inspections of the security vans' collections. After I have issued the collection sheets to the drivers, I pick a number of the shops and go there by car to wait for the relevant van to arrive. I can then observe that the van's crew and the shop's manager or assistant manager are carrying out the security routines properly.

Yesterday I picked two of the Belston shops and observed the crews of Vans 1 and 2 picking up their collections. I had scheduled Van 3 to make a collection on the Orchard Estate at Belston and then pass through

Belstone Lane to pick up at the Bellsich High Street shop.

After visiting Belston I went on to Bellsich High Street and waited in my car outside our shop for Van 3 to arrive. I was there about 15 minutes before they should have got there.

I waited nearly half an hour but Van 3 did not arrive. Eventually I realised that something had gone wrong and I returned to headquarters where I was informed that Van 3 had been attacked and robbed in Belstone Lane and that Driver Morrison and Guard Williams had been injured.

It was signed and dated again at the end.

Next were a batch of statements from residents in Belstone Lane, all very similar:

Name: Arthur Barrett
Age/DOB: 43. 18071937
Occupation: Insurance broker

Then there was the bit about it all being true, then:

I live at 23 Belstone Lane, Bellsich. It is a detached house standing on the east side of the lane in between numbers 21 and 25.

Yesterday was very hot and I spent the afternoon in the garden until it got too hot to stay out. I then went indoors and watched sport on television until tea-time.

After my wife and I had tea we watched a bit more television then I decided to go out and have a drink. I went upstairs to the bathroom to shave and change.

The bathroom is at the head of the stairs, at the front of the house. As I was standing in the bathroom shaving I heard a squeal of brakes outside in the lane. I could not see what had happened because the bathroom window is frosted but I thought that someone had turned off the roundabout on the main road and come into Belstone Lane too fast, as they often do.

I carried on shaving and then I heard shouts outside so I walked through to the bedroom, from where I could look down into the lane.

When I looked out of the bedroom window I saw that a big white transit van was stopped in the lane slightly left from our house. In front of the white transit was a smaller blue van that was stopped at an angle across the front of the transit as though to prevent it getting past. I could also see that there was a red saloon parked behind the white transit, but I could not see all of this vehicle across the top of the transit.

Two men in dark uniforms were standing in the road near the front of the transit. They had their hands in the air because two men were pointing guns at them. The men with the guns were both dressed in dark clothes and wore ski masks. One had a pistol and the other had a shotgun.

The man with the pistol was standing on the far (west) side of the lane. The man with the shotgun was on the near side, standing on the grass verge. When I looked out he was turned around and seemed to be shouting something at someone I couldn't see.

There were other men, I'm not sure how many, taking bags out of the back of the white transit and putting them into the red car.

I knew that the white van was a security van and I realised at once that it was being robbed. I picked up the bedside phone and dialled 999 straight away.

While I was giving the particulars of what was happening I heard a woman's voice call out. Then I heard a big bang and a lot of shouting. As soon as I had completed my call I went straight back to the window.

One of the uniformed men was lying in the road in a pool of blood and there was a big splash of blood across the near side of the white van. I could not see the other uniformed man.

The masked men were jumping into the blue van and the red car. When they were in, both vehicles went off very fast in different directions.

I shouted down to my wife and told her not to go outside and I phoned 999 again to tell them that an ambulance was needed.

A few minutes later the police and an ambulance arrived.

Barrett's neighbours were no more help. Some were indoors, some in their back gardens. None of them actually saw the robbery and the shooting. Most of them only realised that something unusual was happening when the shotgun went off.

Which meant that the prosecution didn't have the best evidence. There was no witness who could point to Walton or Grady and say, 'I saw that man committing robbery and murder.'

Next came a statement from the surviving guard telling how they had been ambushed in Belstone Lane and describing the killing of his partner and the injuries to himself. There were doctors' statements from St Agnes' Hospital in Belston where the guards had been treated and a pathologist's report on the post-mortem. Again – all of it irrelevant, but marvellously prejudicial to a jury.

There were statements from the police officers who were first on the scene. When they got there the robbers had vanished. The driver of the security van was in a bad way after taking both barrels of the shotgun in his hip and thigh. His partner was already dead, killed by a single pistol shot. No witness could identify the robbers or either of their vehicles and no one had a vehicle number.

Road-blocks had been set up, but no vehicle connected with the robbery was stopped. The following day a picnic party on Cannock Chase found the red car parked in a copse, doors wide open. Mantons paperwork scattered inside identified it. It carried false registration plates and a check on the engine block number revealed it to have been stolen from West Bromwich some months before. The blue van was never found. This section of the evidence ended with a statement from a Mantons accountant that the money had never been recovered. Mantons had been reimbursed by their insurers.

That had been the point at which the enquiry jammed eighteen years ago. I put the bundle down and rubbed my eyes. None of it harmed Walton, but none of it helped him. The robbers might have been anyone.

I was about to read on when Sheila returned from shopping. 'It's bejeely cold out,' she said, 'and starting to snow again.'

I stood up. 'Take this pre-warmed chair,' I invited, 'while I make us a warm drink.'

'Beauty!' she exclaimed and fell into the chair while I made off to the kitchen.

'You know something?' she called after me.

'What's that?'

'I suppose I could learn to live in a country where it sleets and snows if all the blokes warm a girl's chair for her.'

I returned with two Gaelic coffees. 'Ah, but it's only public schoolboys who do it,' I said. 'They're trained by having to warm the stone bog seats for their seniors.'

She grabbed a glass, gulped and shivered as the mixture went down. 'On the other hand,' she said, 'some of your ancient traditions are so bizarre as to be perverse.'

'Nonsense,' I said. 'You can't have chaps who are going to spend the rest of their lives on the benches of the House of Commons, the Lords or the courts being disabled by a premature bout of piles or pneumonia.'

'And what about the poor bloody juniors?' she demanded. 'How many of them get premature piles?'

'Ah,' I said. 'The traditional Aussie support of the

underdog. It's a selection process. The weakest go to the wall, the rest go on to serve the nation. Anyway, they're all modernised now – that's why Britain's bankrupt and a third-class power.'

She grimaced at me and began flipping through the bundle of evidence while she drank her coffee.

'Tell me about witness statements,' she said, after a few minutes.

'What about them?' I asked.

'How are they taken?'

'Well, the first police officers at the scene will have checked to see if anyone around saw anything useful. If it had been a small incident they would have taken the witness statements. Since there were a lot of people who saw part of the robbery, they called in a support unit the next day to interview all the witnesses.'

'And how would they have taken them? Were they typed out then?'

'No. The interviewing officers would write them out by hand and the witnesses would sign them on the spot.'

She frowned. 'But these copies are typed.'

'Yes. When the case was prepared for trial they would prepare typescript copies and have the witnesses re-sign them. It's easier on everybody's eyesight not having to peer at policemen's scribbles.'

She looked puzzled. 'What's the problem?' I asked.

'So the original manuscript statement is made and signed on the day after the robbery, eighteen years ago – yes?'

'Yes. That's why they all refer to "yesterday".'

'And then Walton and Grady are charged and the statements are typed up, re-signed and redated – right?'

'Yes.'

'Six years after?'

'Yes.'

'Then it's wrong,' she announced. 'Look!'

She showed me, turning through the pages and pointing

out each date. All of the statements of the Belstone Lane witnesses had been re-signed and dated in the October following the robbery – months after the incident and six years before there was a chance of a trial.

'That doesn't make any kind of sense,' I said. 'It looks as if they were expecting a trial that autumn – but they weren't.'

I pulled out my slip of notes and added one:

Check re-signing of witness statements.

14

That night was 'Macintyre's thrash' as we called it – a private dinner for a few friends at the Victoria Hotel in honour of Scotland's greatest poet, Robbie Burns.

Apart from Sheila and me, my assistant Alasdair Thayne was there, Claude the Phantom, John Parry, and a spattering of other local disreputables whose company amused Mac. He, of course, attended in full regalia – velvet jacket, kilt, lace ruffles, the whole lot except that he wore a scalpel down his stocking-top instead of a knife.

Among the guests I was pleased to see David Lyon, my predecessor as the town's principal legal irritant. After decades of magistrates' court crime and alcohol he had retired to somewhere on the Mediterranean a couple of years before to concentrate on the alcohol.

'Good to see you, David,' I said. 'They told me you were drinking yourself to death in Cyprus or somewhere.'

He smiled. 'It wasn't Cyprus, it was Tunisia, and as to drinking myself to death I've never felt so well in my life.'

'What brings you back to Belston in midwinter?'

'A hankering for the sight of the Black Country under

snow? No – once in a while I have to come and shout at my broker in person or he stops taking me seriously. But what are you doing and who's that delightful freckled lady who came in with you?'

I introduced Sheila and the conversation became more general. Soon Macintyre summoned us to the table, where the Victoria's chefs had done justice to Scottish cuisine by providing huge dishes of mashed potatoes and swedes.

'And now . . .' declaimed the Scots doctor, '. . . the entry of the haggis!'

He flung open the door. Unearthly groans poured into the room, followed by a piper in full dress followed in turn by two of the Victoria's waiters bearing haggis on silver trays and trying hard not to laugh, drop the haggises, or both.

We charged our glasses and Macintyre toasted the haggis, then whipped an unpleasantly large scalpel from his stocking and bent over one of the trays with a determined eye.

Sheila whispered, 'What's the murder weapon?'

'It's a Victorian horse lancet,' I said. 'Belonged to Doc's grandfather.'

She shuddered. 'I hope he wasn't using it this afternoon,' she said.

In rolling Scots tones Macintyre began to declaim the 'Address to the Haggis' . . .

> 'God bless thy honest, sonsy face,
> Great chieftain o' the pudding race . . .'

In a near perfect imitation of Mac's tones, Alasdair Thayne recited quietly, 'Deceased weighed some twenty pounds and was plump and in apparent good health. When examined he was still steaming and was surrounded by what appeared to be mashed potatoes and swedes. Cause of death was not immediately apparent.'

Macintyre shot him a fierce glare but rumbled on to the

end of the address, when his skilled knife slit the steaming haggis from end to end and we lifted our glasses.

Lyon leaned over the table as the haggis was served around. 'John Parry tells me you're lumbered with a late appeal in the Belstone Lane robbery,' he remarked.

'Lumbered's the very word,' I said, and outlined the position. When I told him about the odd dating on the statements he nodded.

'That would be from the trial,' he said.

'But the trial wasn't for six years,' I protested.

'No, no,' he said, 'not the trial of your fellows – the first trial.'

'What first trial?'

'A few months after the robbery they nicked three blokes and charged them – not with the robbery and murder, because they couldn't place them at the scene. But they charged them with conspiracy to rob.'

'What happened?' I asked, amazed at his news.

He smiled. 'I represented them and they got off, of course.'

I gaped. 'But who were they?'

He frowned. 'Now you're asking,' he said. 'It was a long time ago.'

He gazed past my head, straining to recall. 'They were all black,' he said at last, 'but I can't put names to them.'

'Black!' I exclaimed. 'Was one of them Banjo Cook? George Cook?'

He shook his head. 'Doesn't ring any bells,' he said. 'I'll tell you what, I sold out to Graham Lillington. He should still have my old file register. The names'll be in there.'

'What about the file?' I asked, hoping for a miracle.

'Only obliged to keep crime files for two years,' he said.

'But everyone keeps them longer,' I said, still hoping.

'But I had a thorough clear-out before I sold up.

Couldn't have Graham acquiring dark secrets he hadn't paid for, could I? There won't be a file, but Graham should still have the register.'

We turned back to our haggis and the evening pursued its usual course. Macintyre recited reams of Burns, then we sang the unexpurgated versions of 'John Anderson, My Jo' and half a dozen other Burns songs before Mac brought proceedings to a melodramatic climax with a recital of 'Tam O'Shanter' with lantern slides. Usually I relaxed and enjoyed Mac's bizarre entertainment on Burns' Night, but Lyon's information kept dancing among the whisky fumes and whispering possibilities.

Back at home, Sheila slid quickly into bed and dragged me after her. 'I'm cold,' she complained.

'Turn the heating up,' I suggested.

'There's better ways to warm up,' she remarked and proceeded to demonstrate.

Afterwards we lay and smoked. 'Penny for 'em,' she said.

'Are you implying that my mind wasn't on what we were doing?' I demanded.

'It was then,' she said. 'It isn't now. You've been thoughtful all evening.'

I told her about Lyon and the trial of his clients. She looked puzzled. 'Does it help?' she asked.

'I'm damned if I know. The Payday Gang are the obvious suspects, but apparently they didn't do it. Lyon's clients were accused of planning to do it, but they were acquitted, and Walton and Grady say they didn't do it, but they're serving the time.'

'Was George Cook one of Lyon's clients?' she asked.

I shook my head. 'He didn't seem to think so. None of it makes any sense. I'll have to check with Lillington on Monday.'

The bedside phone rang. I groaned. Sheila had been around me long enough to groan with me. A call at this time was most likely a police station calling to summon me to attend a client.

I reached out and switched the answering facility to the speaker. When the recorded message had played there was a pause, then an unfamiliar voice spoke. It was a male, probably middle-aged, and it spoke with a slight accent but without much emphasis.

'Mr Tyroll,' it said, 'you don't seem to understand why Banjo Cook is dead. Let me make it quite clear – if you carry on messing about with the Belstone Lane case, you'll end up the same way – and your Aussie girlfriend.'

My phone number is in the book and I've been phoned and threatened before – usually after pubshut by former clients or their friends. They get heavy and ramble, but this quietly undramatic, sober voice frightened me. This was someone who meant every word.

The caller disconnected. As quickly as I could I dialled 1471, but the caller had withheld their number, of course. Sheila and I looked at each other silently. I rewound the cassette and played the message again.

'What's that accent?' she asked, when we had heard the message again.

'North Midlands, I would guess. The Potteries, somewhere round there.'

'What are you going to do?'

'Report it to John Parry and take good care of you.'

She shivered. 'It's made me cold again,' she said and grinned.

15

Next morning the whisky had evaporated. I woke to find Sheila sitting on the bedside playing the cassette quietly. She looked thoughtful.

'You've no idea who this is?' she asked when she saw that I was awake.

I shook my head. 'The voice means nothing to me, and as to who might threaten us – well, somebody topped George Cook to stop him talking to me. Whoever it is must be the same.'

'So you're going to take it seriously?'

'Sure I am, but it's a bit difficult when you don't know who's attacking. I can't stay in bed and pull the blankets over my head. I've got a living to make and an office to run. All I can do is stay away from dark, lonely places and stop taking sweets from strangers – and you can do the same.'

I dawdled over the Sunday papers as long as I could, but in the end I forced myself back to the boxes of papers on Walton's case. I had read as far as the end of the original incident. Now I wanted to know why it took six years to bring charges and how Glenys Simpson became involved. I had a feeling that I was about to be disappointed and I was.

The story simply started anew after six years. There was no explanation from anyone of how Glenys got into the act, just statements from three Crime Squad officers who had interviewed her when she volunteered to make a statement. I was not surprised that they were Hawkins, Watters and Saffary. Then came her statement:

Name: Glenys Mary Simpson née Whitethorne
Age/DOB: 43. 09101942
Occupation: Housewife
Who states: This statement, consisting of two pages, each signed by me, is true to the best of my knowledge and belief and I make it knowing that if it is tendered in evidence I shall be liable to prosecution if I have wilfully stated in it anything which I know to be false or do not believe to be true.
Dated: 19041986 *Signed*: G. Simpson

I am a divorced woman formerly married to William Arnold Simpson. We separated in 1981 and have been divorced for about three years. I have not remarried.

I have been asked what I know about my former husband's criminal activities. On 19th April 1986 I was interviewed by officers of the Central Midlands police and made a long statement to them about my former husband's involvement in crime. That statement was made at my suggestion and entirely voluntarily.

My interview with the officers was tape-recorded. I have been shown a typed transcript of that interview. I have read that transcript and it is a correct and accurate transcript of the interview. I now produce it as Exhibit GMS/1.

Signed: G. Simpson

That was all. Nothing at all about how she came to shop her ex-husband and his pals six years on from the robbery.

GMS/1 was in a box of exhibited documents, a fat bundle of dog-eared typescript. The beginning should have explained how the interview came about, but it didn't.

Watters: This interview is being recorded in an interview room at Belston police station. Present in the room are myself, Detective Inspector Watters, Detective Chief Inspector Hawkins and PC Stephenson who is in charge of the recording equipment. Also present is Mrs Glenys Simpson. Now, Mrs Simpson, just so we can have things clear on the tape, you are present at this interview voluntarily – entirely of your own free will?

Mrs Simpson: Yes.

Watters: And you are the former wife of William Arnold Simpson?

Mrs Simpson: Yes, that's right.

Watters: And your date of birth is . . . ?

Mrs Simpson: 9th October 1942.

Watters: And your former husband's date of birth is . . . ?

Mrs Simpson: 5th June 1939.

Watters: And you wish to make a statement detailing what you know about the criminal activities of your former husband?

Mrs Simpson: Yes, that's right. I think it's time that all this came out in the open, all that Billy and his mates did.

Watters: And nobody's promised you any reward and nobody's threatened you? This is entirely of your own free will?

Mrs Simpson: That's right.

Hawkins: Right, Glenys, can you tell us a bit about the background, a bit about your marriage to Billy Simpson?

Mrs Simpson: Well, we married in 1960 or '61, I forget which. When we were first married Billy was working at Bowcotts Electrical. He was very clever with electrical things.

Hawkins: Where did you live then, Glenys?

Mrs Simpson: We lived with Billy's parents, out in Bellsich Road, at first. Then we got a council house in Eastern Avenue. We stayed there until we split up.

Hawkins: And who were his friends at that time?

Mrs Simpson: Well, there was people from Bowcotts that he worked with, and he went fishing a lot. There was people he fished with, but there was a little group that he was always knocking about with.

Hawkins: And who were they?

Mrs Simpson: There was Peter Grady . . .

Hawkins: How did he come to know Grady?

Mrs Simpson: Well, he was from Bowcotts, Peter. He was a shop steward there and Billy was keen on the union so I think that's how they met.

Hawkins: And who else was in this little group of Billy's friends?

Mrs Simpson: There was Peter Grady and ■■■■■ ■■■■■■. He was the landlord of the ■■■■■ ■■■■■ at the time and Billy and the others used to drink in there. Then there was Alan Walton. Alan had a lorry and did haulage. He used to drink in the ■■■■■ ■■■■■, too.

Hawkins: And where did they meet, mainly?

Mrs Simpson: Well, mostly they either went to the ■■■■■ ■■■■■ or they met at our house. They used to come back from the pub and Billy would take them into our spare room upstairs. He had a sort of workshop up there where he fixed tellies and things.

Hawkins: And were you present when they met at your home? Did you know what they discussed?

Mrs Simpson: Oh, no. Billy wouldn't have me around with his pals. He always took them straight upstairs. All I had to do was take them more beer or tea when they wanted it.

Hawkins: And how did they let you know if they wanted more beer or a cup of tea, Glenys?

Mrs Simpson: Well, there was this thing in the spare room, like a sort of little telephone.

Hawkins: What was that for?

Mrs Simpson: Well, that room was our babby's room when she was alive. Billy fixed this thing up then, so that we could hear if she cried. It was like a little box at each end with a wire in between. He put one in that room and one in the living-room downstairs.

Hawkins: How did it work exactly?

Mrs Simpson: There was a button on each of the boxes and a speaker. If you pressed the button it buzzed at the other box, but if you just switched the box on you could hear noises at the other end. It was so we could listen to the babby without going upstairs.

Hawkins: Let me get this right. Billy installed an intercom in the living-room with the other end in the spare bedroom – his workshop, where he used to meet with his mates? Is that right?

Mrs Simpson: That's right.

Hawkins: And this intercom could be switched on from either end so that you could listen to sounds at the other end?

Mrs Simpson: That's it, yes.

Hawkins: And that's what Billy used to give you messages to bring him and his pals more tea or beer when they were in the spare room?

Stephenson: Sorry, Mrs Simpson, but you'll have to give a spoken answer. The tape can't record nods.

Mrs Simpson: Oh, yes, of course. Yes, that's right. He used to push the buzzer and ask for tea or beer or sandwiches.

Hawkins: I don't suppose you cared very much for being left out and having to do all the fetching and carrying and brewing up?

Mrs Simpson: No, I bloody didn't. Sometimes when Billy brought them in during the day I used to go out, just so as not to have to run his bloody messages like a skivvy.

Hawkins: How often did they get together in Billy's workshop?

Mrs Simpson: Well, at first it was just once or twice a week then there was the big strike at Bowcotts and they was in there every afternoon and most nights. Like I said, Peter Grady was a shop steward. He was a Communist, they say he started the strike. By then Billy was on the union committee. They'd go to meetings down at the ■■■■■ ■■■■■, then they'd come back to our place and settle down in the spare room for hours on end.

Hawkins: When was the Bowcotts strike?

Mrs Simpson: 1976. Right through that winter into the next year. Then when it was over, Billy and Grady and the other union men was shoved out as soon as Bowcotts could. After that he never had a job again.

Hawkins: So in 1976 and '77 they spent a lot of time in Billy's workshop and you think they were talking about the strike at Bowcotts?

Mrs Simpson: That's it, yes.

Hawkins: After the strike was over, as you say, Billy and Pete Grady lost their jobs at Bowcotts. Did they spend much time in the workshop then?

Mrs Simpson: Oh, when they hadn't got no jobs to go to, they was always in there, day and night.

Hawkins: And did you wonder what it was they were talking about now the strike was over?

Mrs Simpson: I did.

Hawkins: And did you find out?

Mrs Simpson: Yes, I did in the end.

Hawkins: How did that come about?

Mrs Simpson: Well, they was all upstairs one day and I was downstairs, doing a bit of tidying in the living-room. I must have caught the switch on that telephone box thing . . .

Watters: The intercom to the workshop?

Mrs Simpson: That's right. I must have knocked the switch because it came on and I could hear their voices coming through it.

Hawkins: And what were they talking about?

Mrs Simpson: Well, I was going to switch it off again, but I heard Peter Grady talking about guns.

Hawkins: Did that surprise you?

Mrs Simpson: Not really. He was always going on about guns. He was always saying as we'd never have a decent government in this country by voting them in. He used to say that we'd have to get guns and change the government by force.

Hawkins: And is that the kind of thing that he was saying when you accidentally switched the intercom on?

Mrs Simpson: Well, no. I could hear that he was actually talking about collecting some guns from somewhere to do a job.

I had never liked the late Hawkins; he was always a great deal too flash and arrogant for my taste, but I had to admire this interview. It certainly wasn't an off-the-cuff session with someone who just wandered into a police station and wanted to unburden themselves. Hawkins evidently knew exactly what Glenys Simpson had to say and was very carefully making sure that she said it in the right order. I was about to ask Sheila for another Gaelic coffee when I had a guilty recollection of Glenys Simpson ferrying trays of tea and cans of beer up the stairs to the back bedroom. I didn't know whether she was telling the truth or not, but I fetched my own coffee before turning back to the transcript.

Hawkins: Did Grady actually talk about a 'job'?
Mrs Simpson: Yes, that's what he said. I didn't understand at first.
Watters: But you carried on listening?
Mrs Simpson: Well, yes. It was the talk about guns and I wanted to know what they wanted guns for.
Hawkins: And did you find out?
Mrs Simpson: Peter Grady was saying that he could get the guns they'd need . . .
Watters: Did he say where the guns would come from?
Mrs Simpson: No. He only said that he'd got a contact and he could get the guns they'd need.
Hawkins: Was that all that was said about the guns?
Mrs Simpson: Yes. After that they started talking about where and when they were going to do whatever it was.
Hawkins: And where was that?
Mrs Simpson: I think that one was a payroll van in Erdington, wasn't it?
Watters: You'll have to tell us what you remember, Mrs

Simpson, but there was a robbery on a payroll van in Erdington.

Hawkins: And you believe that was what they were discussing the first time you overheard them?

Mrs Simpson: Yes, I think that was the one.

Hawkins: After that time, were there other occasions when you used the intercom to listen in on Billy and his mates?

Mrs Simpson: Oh, after that I did it regular.

Watters: And it was always the same group – your husband, Grady, ■■■■■ and Walton?

Mrs Simpson: That's right.

Hawkins: Tell us about some of the other things you overheard.

Hang on a minute, Mr Hawkins! What about the Erdington job? He'd just leapt right over it. There were no details in the transcript apart from the fact that the group had discussed the job and Grady had said he could get the guns from a contact. Why hadn't they asked about Simpson's movements on the day of the robbery? Why hadn't they asked any more about what she overheard? When and where the van was to be stopped? Who was actually going to do it? Where were the vehicles they used going to come from?

All Hawkins had was a bare outline and he hadn't paused to fill it in before pressing on for further information about other jobs. I stopped reading and riffled through the thick bundle to see if Erdington was ever mentioned again. It wasn't.

16

I read on. Glenys Simpson had claimed to have heard her husband and his mates planning about a dozen major robberies. In each case the response of Hawkins and his team was the same. Once she'd mentioned where the job was they pressed on to the next one. Not once did they pause to collect any detail from her that could be used to tie Billy Simpson and his pals to any of the crimes. Not until they reached Belstone Lane, that is.

Hawkins: You overheard mention of the Mantons van?

Mrs Simpson: Yes. They was going to do it on a Saturday night and I remember thinking that Saturday night was a funny time for a payroll van to be about.

Hawkins: And what did they say about the Mantons van?

Mrs Simpson: They said as they should do it in hot weather, 'cos it would be carrying a lot more. Peter said he'd find the guns. Alan and ■■■■■ were going to fix up a van and a car . . .

Watters: They said a van and a car. That was part of their plan – to use a van and a car?

Mrs Simpson: Yes. Alan said he knew where there was a van they could use and scrap it afterwards. ■■■■■ said he'd have no trouble getting a car.

Hawkins: Do you remember the evening of the Belstone Lane robbery, Glenys?

Mrs Simpson: I'll never forget it. Billy went out in the afternoon, about three. I thought I'd go out later, for a drink with a neighbour of mine. We went to the Miners Arms and heard it on the telly, how they'd killed one chap and injured another. I was really sick, I can tell you. I can remember sitting in that pub and there was people saying as they should bring back hanging and I sat there thinking, 'My husband done that! My Billy and his mates! They ain't just thieves – they'm murderers!'

Hawkins: And what did you do then?

Mrs Simpson: I went home at pubshut. They was all there – the four of them. They'd parked a van on the waste ground behind and carried stuff up the gulley into the house.

Watters: Did you see the van, Mrs Simpson?

Mrs Simpson: Ah, it were a scruffy old dark blue transit. I don't know what make it would have been.

Watters: And all four of them were in the house?

Mrs Simpson: Yes, all of them.

Hawkins: How were they dressed?

Mrs Simpson: Well, you know how hot the weather had been, but they was all wearing jackets, all dark jackets.

Watters: You said they carried stuff from the van – what sort of stuff?

Mrs Simpson: It was all there. There was guns, there was balaclava things, black ones, and there was cash bags all over the table. They was counting the money out when I come in.

Hawkins: What happened when you came in?

Mrs Simpson: Well, I couldn't believe it. They'd gone out and shot a man dead and they'd come back to my house. I yelled at Billy. I said, 'Do you know you've killed a man, you bastard!' He said, 'He ain't dead, either of them.' I said, 'It was on the telly. You've killed one man and maybe another!'

Hawkins: What did he say?

Mrs Simpson: He said, 'It went wrong. It weren't our fault. Now shut up and help get this money sorted.'

Hawkins: And what did you do?

Mrs Simpson: I dain't have no choice, did I? I helped them sort the money out. Then Alan and ■■■■■ took the cash bags and the dark jackets and the balaclava things, to get rid of them and the van, and Peter took the guns.

Watters: What happened to the money?

Mrs Simpson: Billy had that. He made me help him hide it.

Watters: Where was it hidden?

Mrs Simpson: We had an old shed at the back, Billy used to keep his fishing stuff there and that. It had a dirt floor. We went out there and he shovelled up a bit of the floor in the shed and there was one of those, like old-fashioned metal signs, like they used to have on shops, and underneath that was a hole. He put all the money in the hole and put that metal sheet on top of it and put the dirt back. Then we trampled it down and he spilled oil and things on it so it looked like it hadn't been dug up.

Hawkins: Do you know what Billy did with the money afterwards?

Mrs Simpson: No. He never told me. He just said as it warn't in the shed any more.

Watters: When was that? When did he say that?

Mrs Simpson: Only about a day or two after. After the police had been.

Hawkins: Right, the police came. Do you remember when that was, Glenys?

Mrs Simpson: Do I remember? Course I do! It was the next day – the Sunday, late in the morning. There was masses of them.

Watters: What happened when they came?

Mrs Simpson: Well, they said to Billy as they knew he'd planned the job and they thought he'd done it as well. They asked him about his whereabouts on the Saturday night.

Watters: What did he say?

Mrs Simpson: He was one of them (*indicating Det/Insp. Watters*). He can tell you what went on.

Hawkins: Yes, Glenys, but this has to be what you remember.

Mrs Simpson: Oh, right. Well, they searched the house, every inch, top to bottom, and they kept on at us about where we was on the Saturday evening. Billy said as he was in a pub in Wednesbury with his mates. I said what was true, that I had gone out for a drink with me neighbour. Billy had told me to say that he came home alone, after I got home, so I told them that.

Hawkins: But that wasn't true. Why did you tell the officers what wasn't true?

Mrs Simpson: I hadn't no choice, had I? Billy had killed a bloke. I dain't know what he might do to me if I spoke out.

Hawkins: Right, you followed his instructions out of fear. Is there anything more you can recall about the Belstone Lane robbery?

Mrs Simpson: No, no. That's all I can remember. Sometimes I wish I could forget.

That was all, but it was enough for Hawkins' purposes. She had Billy and his pals planning the job, obtaining the vehicles and the guns, coming back afterwards with the loot, the weapons, the clothing, the van, getting rid of the evidence, hiding the loot, and Billy instructing her to say he came home alone. It was a first-class basis on which to go out and arrest the four – if she was telling the truth.

17

'It all looks phoney to me,' Sheila said, after she'd looked over the transcript.

'Why's that?'

'They're putting on a show for the tape. She's been rehearsed.'

'You think so?'

'Sure of it, cobber. She and Hawkins have been over what she's going to say. Then he presents her story, leading her into it the right way. Watters is the technician who nails down the little details. It's a phoney. And what about Saffary?'

'How do you mean?'

'Well, isn't it funny he wasn't there?'

'Who knows why he wasn't there – he could have been on leave or out mugging pensioners but they covered his interest anyway.'

She raised a questioning eyebrow.

'Saffary's a dyed-in-the-wool bigot,' I explained. 'He hates foreigners of all kinds, Catholics, Jews, Labour Party members, blacks, Asians, moderate Tories and me. Grady was a shop steward with a reputation as a Communist. When Saffary knew that she had said that Grady had the contact that supplied the guns he would have thought he was on the track of the world-wide Communist conspiracy and that plane-loads of weapons were being flown into Belston every night. He'd have been less than pleased if it hadn't been pushed.'

Sheila nodded. 'I take it', she said, 'that the black bits that have been blanked out are references to Freddy Hughes?'

'Certainly.'

'So why have they been covered up?'

'When someone started this game with Glenys, the idea seems to have been that she would play the conscience-stricken former wife thereby giving Hawkins' gang an excuse to go for Billy and his pals. That's why she put all their names in. Then, when they arrest Grady, Walton and Hughes, Freddy can't be put in the frame for some reason. It's too late to alter her evidence – a tape and a transcript exist – so they merely blank Hughes out of the version put forward at the trial. It's quite usual to conceal names in witness statements at a trial. If Hughes' name had been in front of the jury, defence counsel could have played hell with the coppers in the witness box – "Who is Freddy Hughes? Why isn't he in the dock? Oh, you arrested him at the same time but you didn't charge him? Why was that? What's the difference between Mr Hughes and my client?" Enough of that kind of thing and even a jury might have smelt a rat.'

'Then why didn't the defence call him? Grady and Walton must have told their lawyers who the fourth man was.'

'Of course they must, but they may not have been able to find him. We can't find him at the moment. And anyway, they needed to be sure of his explanation as to why he walked out when his mates were charged. Added to which they needed to be damned sure that Hughes wasn't in the Belstone Lane job. You don't call a witness unless you are absolutely certain what he's going to say – not only to you, but under cross-examination.'

'There's the other thing, too,' she said.

'What's that?'

'Why'd she do it? For years she knows, so she says, that her old man's running a gang of armed robbers and she says nothing. Then she knows they've killed a bloke. Still she says nothing. Then they split up, then they divorce, then – a couple of years after – she finally decides to dob him in. It doesn't make any kind of sense.'

It was my turn to nod. 'Right. It would have made more sense if all this had come out when they split up or in the course of the divorce. Then there's the attitude of Hawkins' merry men.'

'How do you mean?'

'It's not just that it reads like a prepared presentation. This is big stuff, right? This is a witness who is giving them the lowdown on a dozen armed robberies and a murder. Your average Crime Squad man would have been ramping at his lead like a Rottweiler, but what do this lot do? They sit around while she recites her list of jobs that Billy and the lads planned and executed and they barely ask a question.'

I flipped the pages of the transcript bundle. 'Look here! She's telling them about a robbery in Erdington, one in

Sutton Coldfield, one at North Bromwich, at Walsall, Wolverhampton – blags all over the area. And they're not paying a blind bit of attention. Where's Inspector Watters with his determination to get the details right? They took her right through Belstone Lane, from what she heard of the planning to the hiding of the loot to the police search, and even asked if there was anything else she remembered. But that's the only one. All the others they ignored the details.'

'Why do you think that was?'

'Because Belstone Lane was an unsolved murder. All the others – I suspect – were put down to the Payday Gang and they were convicted. So, if they took notice of what she said about Erdington and Sutton and the rest, either they'd convicted a load of the wrong men as the Payday Gang or Billy Simpson and his mates were a part of the Payday Gang that was never convicted. Far easier to leave the others lie and concentrate on Belstone Lane. That was one where they still needed somebody to convict.'

'It's still odd, though,' she mused. 'If somebody – say Hawkins – set her up to act as the informer why is she giving them stories about crimes they don't want to know about?'

'Two agendas,' I suggested. 'Hawkins simply wants her to trot out chapter and verse about Belstone Lane, but she's got a head of steam up about Billy. This is her big chance to nail him once and for all. Everybody in the Midlands could have recited that list of robberies. She's simply over-egging the pudding and because of the tape and PC Stephenson, Hawkins can't tell her to shut up and concentrate on Belstone Lane. After all, Stephenson isn't one of the gang – he isn't even a CID man, he's a wally.'

'A wally?'

'A uniformed constable, not a detective constable. "Wally" is a term that the CID uses for its uniformed colleagues. They also call them "woolly-pullies" from the blue matchlock sweaters that the uniformed branch wear.'

She shook her head slowly in wonderment at the niceties of English class attitudes. After a moment she said, 'You're going to need to track down Hughes, aren't you? And you need to know about the Payday Gang's trial.'

'That'll be in the newspaper files. John Parry says they were tried in Brum about 1981. It'll be in the papers.'

Sheila looked thoughtful. 'Tell me,' she said, 'do you believe Walton's innocent now?'

'You keep asking me that. I've told you – I'm not even expected to consider his innocence. I have to act on his instructions unless I personally know they're not true.'

'Don't come the raw prawn with me, Chris Tyroll! It matters to me – now, what do you think?'

'If he isn't innocent, why the fake evidence to convict him? Why the lies in the Court of Appeal? Why threats to me?'

'Well, think about this,' she said. 'On the day after the robbery, the Crime Squad landed on Billy Simpson's door-step. Why?'

'The police will never say. They'll just say that they were "acting on information received".'

'So, in other words, it wasn't just darling Glenys who thought Billy Simpson was an armed robber all the way back then? Was it?'

18

We were both right. Sheila was right to question why the police thought Billy Simpson was an armed robber at the time of the Belstone Lane job and I was right that there was going to be no explanation in the papers I had. In fact there was no mention of the raid on the Simpsons' house apart from the reference in Glenys Simpson's statement.

The official story carried on with the statements of officers who had arrested Grady and Walton, about four days after Glenys's interview – time enough for the tape to be transcribed and decisions to be taken. Again – no reference to the arrest of Hughes let alone Billy Simpson.

Alan Walton and Peter Grady had been interrogated for hours. Walton, whether he was guilty or innocent, had said nothing of any consequence. He had kept repeating that he knew nothing about the robbery and that he and Simpson were in a pub in Wednesbury at the time. It had been before the Police and Criminal Evidence Act, when solicitors in interviews were a rarity and statements were handwritten, not tape-recorded. Not that it makes a lot of difference – nowadays they just soften a suspect up before he gets into the interview room and the tape goes on.

Peter Grady's alleged confession was among the exhibits:

> I want to make a statement about my involvement in the Belstone Lane robbery. I have been told that I can write it myself but I want someone to write down what I say.
>
> It was Billy Simpson who got me involved in the robbery. I met Billy when he came to work at Bowcotts. I was the Chairman of the Shop Stewards' Committee and he was an active member of the union. Eventually he was elected on to the committee and we became friends.
>
> The union used to have some of its meetings at the Black Horse in Severn Street and Billy and I used to have a drink together after meetings.
>
> Often when the pub had shut we would go back to Billy's place. At that time he was still living with his wife, Glenys, in a council house in Eastern Avenue.
>
> There was another man who used to go to Billy's with

us. His name was Alan Walton and he had some kind of haulage business. He was an old friend of Billy's. I think they had been at school together.

Billy had a sort of workshop in his house. It was in the back bedroom. He used to fix people's tellies and that. When we went to his place we used to go into that room. At first when we went there we just used to sit around and talk. A lot of our talk was politics and union matters. Billy was more left than me. He used to say that we would never get a decent government by voting for it, that we'd have to have a revolution in England. Sometimes he would say that the working class would have to take away the money from the rich. He used to sing a bit of an American song about how 'The banks are made of marble with a guard at every door, and their vaults are crammed with silver that the workers sweated for'.

Billy's wife was never with us when we talked in Billy's workshop. Sometimes she wasn't in the house if we went there in the day. When we went in the evenings she was usually there, but she never joined us.

Billy had a thing fixed up in his workshop like a sort of intercom. I think it was a thing for listening to the baby that they used to have. It had a buzzer on it and a speaker and when Glenys was downstairs Billy used to buzz it and speak to her to bring us beer or tea and sandwiches. I don't know if she could listen to us from downstairs on it. I suppose she must have been able to because it had been for listening to the baby when it was upstairs.

At first when we went to Billy's we talked about all sorts of things, fishing and football and the union. When the strike was on at Bowcotts we spent a lot of time talking about the strike. After the strike was over Bowcotts got rid of all the activists in the union as soon as they could. There was supposed to be no reprisals but they found ways of getting rid of us and both Billy and me were made redundant.

I had a decent bit of redundancy money, but Billy hadn't been at Bowcotts long and he didn't get much. After he'd been on the dole for a while he really began to feel the pinch. He made a bit with fixing electrical things for people but he started to talk about ways of making money. Every time we were together he would start talking about doing a robbery. At first it was like he was joking but then he seemed to get serious.

Somehow we went along with him. I suppose none of us were doing very well. Alan Walton had lost his licence on a breathalyser and my redundancy money was all gone. We all reckoned that some extra money would come in handy and somehow Billy seemed so convincing.

One day he told us about the Mantons van that picked up the takings from all their shops. He said that they always sent three vans to Belston and they went round the shops in a different order but the last one to finish its round always went through Belstone Lane towards Bellsich to pick up in the High Street there. He said it would be a doddle to stop it in Belstone Lane.

I remember I said that there's houses all along Belstone Lane but Billy said that wouldn't matter. He said we'd have to be armed to threaten the driver and guard on the van and that no one on Belstone Lane would tackle armed men.

I wasn't very happy about guns, but Billy said we'd got to have them to threaten the guards. He said he could get the guns but he never said where.

The longer we talked about it the more it seemed like it would work and Billy kept saying that no one would get hurt, that the security men weren't paid to be heroes and once they saw the guns they'd do what we said. When the really hot weather came we agreed we'd have a go.

We knew pretty close what time the van was due along Belstone Lane and we met at the other end of

Bellsich about an hour before. Billy was in a blue van and Alan was driving a red car. In the van Billy had dark jackets and ski masks and gloves for all of us and he had the guns in his car. There was two shotguns and two pistols. He never said where he got them. There was another bloke with Billy.

I don't know who he was. Billy just said to call him 'Freddy'.

We changed our clothes and Billy and Alan went in the blue van and me and Freddy went in the car. Billy had a shotgun, so did Freddy. Alan and I had the pistols. I have never fired any kind of gun and I wouldn't have known how to use it but I never told them that.

We waited in the car at the Belston end of the lane and Billy waited in the van on the lay-by near the Belsich roundabout. Alan stood at the corner of Belstone Lane and the main road. The plan was that we would follow the Mantons van when it came past us and stay behind it. When Alan saw it come along Belstone Lane he would signal Billy and Billy would bring the blue van into the lane and block the Mantons van. Freddy and I would pull up across the back of it to stop it backing up.

Everything went OK at first. The Mantons van was on time and we followed it. As it got near the end of Belstone Lane the blue van came into the lane and blocked it. Freddy pulled our car across the road behind and we all got out with the guns.

The driver and his mate got out of the Mantons van when they saw the guns. Billy and Alan was at the front telling the driver to open the back. He did that and we started putting cash bags in the car and in our van while Billy and Alan kept guns on the driver and his mate. Billy was standing out in the road with a pistol pointed at the driver's mate and Alan was standing on the grass verge with a shotgun pointed at the driver.

Freddy and me was busy shifting the cash bags and I

> heard an old woman yelling something and Alan yelling back. The next I knew was Alan's shotgun going off and then Billy firing his pistol. I saw the driver go down and there was blood everywhere all up the side of the Mantons van. I didn't know if he was dead. Billy was yelling at us to get a move on so we piled everything in the car and the van and we took off.

They had gone in different directions, the car heading back along the lane into Belston and the van leaving through Bellsich. They used roundabout routes to reach their rendezvous point on Cannock Chase, where they changed out of their clothing, put all the cash bags in the van and abandoned the red car. Then they made for Billy Simpson's place. After that his statement agreed with Glenys Simpson's as to the sorting of the money. Grady claimed to know nothing about where the money was hidden. He had received his share months later, from Simpson. He had never been questioned by the police about the matter before. The document ended with what they call the 'caption' – a paragraph in the suspect's own handwriting:

> The above statement, consisting of eleven pages each signed by me, is true and I make it of my own free will. I have read it over and I have been told that I can add, alter or correct anything which I wish.

Before they started tape-recording statements they used to make the suspect add that paragraph and sign it. They would give them a printed card to copy it out. I've seen guys who could barely write their own name painstakingly copying the card, letter by letter, as though it was Egyptian hieroglyphics, and cheerfully signing to say that they'd read their statements when they couldn't read anything more complicated than a *Sun* headline.

I passed Grady's statement to Sheila without comment and picked up the last few prosecution papers.

The rest of the file was routine stuff, tying up loose ends. A cashier from Mantons produced a schedule showing how much had been collected from each shop on Van 3's run and stated that the money had never been recovered and Mantons had been reimbursed by their insurers. There was a statement by the bloke who took over the Simpsons' old council house. He confirmed that, when he moved in, there was a baby alarm wired from the downstairs front room to the back bedroom upstairs. He had taken it out, but there were photographs exhibited, showing the marks where it had been screwed to the woodwork. He also said that, when he moved the old shed in the garden, he had found an old Tizer enamelled advertising sign in the dirt floor and that there was a big hole underneath it. It wasn't the only big hole around – no mention of Hughes' arrest, no mention of any attempt to arrest Simpson, no mention of his death, no mention of three other blokes who'd been charged with conspiring to rob the Mantons van. The police had carefully tied up the little loose ends, but the big ones were still flapping about.

I brewed the coffee while Sheila read Grady's statement. When I brought the glasses back to her she was frowning at the papers.

'Well?' I said.

'I've read Grady's so-called confession. Why didn't they charge Alan with shotgunning the Mantons guard? Grady says he did.'

'Grady's statement says so, but that's part of the police come-on, isn't it? Can't you imagine it? "Just make a statement and we'll see that it lets you out of the murder and the shotgunning." '

She nodded. 'Yeah, I suppose so, but it lets Alan Walton in for it. Why didn't they charge him?'

'Because you can't be convicted on the unsupported evidence of an accomplice, and there wasn't any evidence to back up Grady's statement.'

'So Walton's lucky? Yes? What would attempted murder or whatever it was get him?'

'Anything up to life.'

She grinned sardonically. 'I wonder if he realises how lucky he is,' she said, then she swept a hand over the bundles of paper. 'Is this absolutely all the evidence that the police had pulled together in six years?'

'No,' I said. 'From the witness statements taken at the time, the evidence arising from Glenys's sudden attack of conscience and the statements of Walton and Grady, they have selected what they think will impress a jury. They've also added a few explanatory bits, like the plan-drawer and the cashier and so on. All the prosecution has to do is present to the jury sufficient evidence to convict – and they did, didn't they? It doesn't have to be all the evidence and it doesn't have to be good evidence. It's up to the defence to test it and see if it's good.'

She sipped the hot liquid and the frown relaxed a little. 'Why doesn't Grady's confession match Glenys Simpson's evidence?'

'Good question. They can't both be telling the truth, can they?'

'No,' she agreed. 'She says that Billy and the boys planned and executed a whole string of bail-ups. He says that Belstone Lane was a one-off. Somebody's lying.'

'Maybe both of them,' I suggested.

'But how did a jury convict both of them on this rubbish?' she demanded.

'Quite easily,' I said. 'Glenys Simpson said that she knew all about the planning of the job by her husband and his mates. Peter Grady was interviewed and admitted that he was involved and implicated the others. Bingo!'

'But didn't anyone draw attention to the differences in court? Were the defence barristers asleep?'

'I don't suppose so,' I said, and dug into one of the document boxes, pulling out a plain blue notebook.

'What's that?'

'This'll be the note of the evidence that Walton's solicitor kept during the trial.'

I thumbed through it until I found Glenys Simpson's name, then looked for a note of the cross-examination by the defence. Solicitors' clerks don't usually write shorthand, they use personal variations on what used to be called 'telegraphers' code' and nowadays is 'reporters' shorthand'. It looks like gibberish.

'Look,' I said, and showed Sheila the relevant note:

Nt spkng out f malce
Nt fr any rwrd
Bcse its rt – wntd t tll trth t lst
1210 hrs.
Xd (Walton)
Kn G mde stmnt to pol.
Dnt kn f its dffrnt t mine
(Given G stmnt t read)
Y – dffrnt
Dnt kn why – wsnt thr whn G sd it
Y – I hrd B & co tlkng abt lots f robbrys
Y – G sys nly 1
G lyng – there was mre
F in Gs sttmnt is FH
(Prosn. appls to keep FH out – J agrs)

'What', Sheila demanded, 'is this nonsense?'

'The clerk with Walton's barrister is noting the evidence. He's not keeping a complete transcript – he's not fast enough – but he's mixing question and answer together in his note, to get the gist of what was said and the sequence of questions. This page has the end of the prosecutor examining Glenys – that's called "evidence in chief" – and at the top of the page he's wrapping her story up tidily with a last assurance that she's only there out of her high regard for the truth. Look, it says, "I'm not speaking out of malice – It's not for any reward – Because it's right – I wanted to tell the truth at last." Then he notes the time when she finished her evidence in chief and it goes on, "1210 hrs. Cross-examined for Walton – I know Grady made a statement to the police – I don't know if it's different to mine" – then she's given Grady's statement to read, then "Yes, it's different – I don't know why, I wasn't there when Grady said it – Yes, I heard Billy & Co talking about lots of robberies – Yes, Grady says only one – Grady's lying – there was more – Freddy in Grady's statement is Freddy Hughes." And at this point the prosecutor leaps up and points out that Grady hasn't said in his statement that Freddy is Hughes, that it's not for Glenys to say what Grady meant and that there is no witness or defendant called Freddy Hughes and it would be far better not to confuse the jury. The judge agrees – of course.'

'But I thought you said that Grady's confession wasn't evidence against Walton?'

'Quite right – that's what the law says. But put yourself in the place of that jury. They're trying what seems to be a particularly callous crime, murder and maiming by a gang intent on stealing cash. They've seen those bloody photographs. They've seen the surviving guard give his evidence from a wheelchair. Then Mrs S stands up – the frightened wife, now prepared to ease her conscience by telling all – she's easy for a jury to believe. Then Grady has his confession shoved in his face and says he never made it, that the police faked it. Well, as a famous whore once remarked, he would say that, wouldn't he?'

'But Alan Walton never confessed – never admitted anything,' she persisted.

'Fair enough. But the jury have heard Grady's statement, saying that Walton was deeply involved. Oh yes, the judge will have warned them that anything Grady said about Alan wasn't evidence against him, but do you imagine for a moment that the jury could consider the case against Walton without recalling Grady's statement? Of course not!'

'It's a swindle!' she said.

'Sure it is, but it looks good on paper. Go to the Court of Appeal and say that they should have been tried separately and they'll say, "But it clearly shows in the transcript that the trial judge warned the jury in the strongest terms that Grady's statement wasn't evidence against Walton." '

She frowned again. 'You're in a dirty business, Chris.'

'You think I don't know it? You got any nice jobs in Oz? Something decent and well-paid, like digging ditches or humping boxes?'

She grinned and squeezed my biceps. 'I don't know about digging ditches,' she said, 'but let's have a trial run at the humping.'

19

It was still snowing in the morning and I tried to persuade Sheila that she really didn't need to go to London for her research. She insisted, announcing that if the snow hadn't broken by tea-time she'd stay overnight in London. I tried to dissuade her by reminding her of the threatening call.

'I'm not going to get mugged in the Public Records Office,' she grinned, 'except by some other researcher who wants what I've got.'

'Just take care,' I said. 'That threat was against you as well as me. Don't take any stupid chances, OK?'

I went into the office with a list of things to do. I had no morning appointments so I called John Parry and told him about Saturday night's threatening call. He came over and listened to the tape.

'And you don't know the voice?' he asked, when he had heard the recording twice.

'No. I think the accent is somewhere around the Potteries, north Staffordshire.'

He nodded. 'And what do you propose to do about it?'

'Isn't that what I'm supposed to ask you? Except that I know that there's not much you can do about it.'

He looked at me expressionlessly. 'There's nothing the police can do until someone tries to implement the threat apart from advising you.'

'And what are you going to tell me? I can't give up the case. I can't stop working in this office. I can't stop going to courts. I can't change where I live.'

'He sounded serious,' said Parry, looking at the cassette. 'Nothing melodramatic, just a straight threat.'

'After last summer,' I said, 'you don't have to teach me to take threats seriously, but what can I do?'

'Well,' he said, 'you're not going to give up the case, so you'll have to be extra careful – keep away from lonely places, stay in company if you can, maintain security here and at your home.'

'This place was resecured after last year's adventures,' I said. 'The house could do with a bit of thought.'

'I'll come and look it over,' he said, 'make a few recommendations.'

'Thanks,' I said. 'Tell me, John, where do you think that threat comes from?'

'You want the theoretical answer? Logic says that, if someone's cage is rattled by you reviving Walton's appeal, then Walton may be innocent. If he is then there's someone out there who got away with murder and robbery. That's who threatened you?'

'And who might that be?'

He shook his big head. 'Now you're asking, boyo. You say that headquarters screwed up the appeal hearing, so it looks like someone in the force has got an interest in it, but you know us – we don't go about issuing anonymous threats. We issue official threats and then lock you up if you upset us.'

I knew too damned well – that was exactly what Saffary had tried to do to me last year.

'The Payday Gang?' I said.

He pursed his lips. 'Why should it be? On the face of it they didn't do Belstone.'

'What about the other three who were tried for conspiracy to rob the Mantons van?'

He looked blank. 'Who were they?'

'Three clients of David Lyon's who were done in the autumn after the robbery. Charged with conspiracy only.'

'Really?' he said. 'I've never heard of that before. What happened to them?'

'Lyon got them off.'

'Who were they? Do you know?'

'No. David's memory didn't stretch that far, but he says that Lillington got his old file register. I'll get him to dig it out.'

That was my next task after John left. Graham Lillington was helpful but admitted that he didn't know where Lyon's old register was. He suggested that I call at his office and he would detach an articled clerk to help me search.

I walked across the square to his office straightaway where he handed me over to an amiable young man who introduced me to their archives. If you think that solicitors are intelligent and logical, try a look at their dead-filing systems. Attics and cellars crammed with damp, dusty, disintegrating files in no particular kind of order. Graham's clerk led me down to their cellar, and switched on the light so I could take in the scope of the problem.

'Which file was it you were looking for, Mr Tyroll?' he asked.

'Not a file,' I said. 'The old file register from David Lyon's firm when your boss bought him out.'

He looked a bit more hopeful. 'Any idea what it looked like?'

'I think it was a big, old-fashioned leather-bound job. I don't know if it had anything on the cover.'

We peered at shelves in the light of a dusty sixty watt bulb. There were rows of old appointment diaries, shelves of out-of-date copies of *Stone's Justices' Manual* and *Archbold's Criminal Pleading*, the Supreme Court Practice and the County Court Practice, a row of Graham's post books, a *Road Traffic Encyclopedia* that seemed to have been run over, several volumes of the 1960 edition of *Halsbury's Laws of England* and, at last, a fat leather-bound ledger with no title.

Coughing in the dust I opened it. On the fly-leaf was a rubber stamp, 'David Lyon, Solicitor & Commissioner for Oaths', and underneath a handwritten title – 'Client Files from 1st January 1975'.

Taking it upstairs I ploughed through it in Graham's waiting-room, looking for three robbery clients in the autumn after the Belstone Lane job. I found them:

100613 Truman, Arnold Conspiracy to Rob,
44 Mill End, Belston. (see 100614/5)
100614 Truman, Leonard Conspiracy to Rob,
3 Park Place, Belston (see 100613/5)
100615 White, Benjamin Conspiracy to Rob,
7 Park Place, Belston (see 100613/4)

They were bracketed together in the last column with a note, 'Paid & Closed, February 1981', so they would have been tried sometime around Christmas of 1980. I jotted down the details of names and addresses, asked Graham's receptionist to thank him for me and headed back to my own office.

Back at my own desk I looked out my scribbled slip of notes:

The Payday Gang?
Freddy Hughes?
Glenys Simpson?
When/How did Hawkins die?
Ring magazine.

Now I could add a couple of entries:

Truman, Truman & White.
Threats with a Potteries accent.

After which it seemed like time to start doing something about them. I called in my articled clerk, Alan Reilly, and despatched him to search the files of the *Evening Mail* and the *Express and Star* for coverage of the Belstone Lane incident, the trial of Truman, Truman and White, and the trial of the Payday Gang.

When he had gone I rang the newspaper whose Sunday supplement had said that Hawkins and Watters had been disciplined for faking interview evidence. Their chief crime reporter had written the article. He quickly set my mind at rest. From somewhere he had obtained copies of the actual disciplinary charges laid against Hawkins and Watters and he read them over to me. There was not a shadow of doubt that they had been accused and found guilty of faking a confession in the Hussain case. The standard of proof in police disciplinary matters is the same as in a criminal court – 'beyond reasonable doubt' – so, in effect, they had been found guilty of forgery.

I called Claude the Phantom on his mobile and gave him a list of people to find, but not to approach – Freddy Hughes, Glenys Simpson, the Trumans, Benjamin White and, as an afterthought, any friends or relatives of Billy Simpson.

For a few minutes afterwards I actually thought I was getting a grip on Walton's case, but it was only a few minutes before I realised that I was simply doing things without really knowing why and without the least idea what results they might produce. I pulled some files out of my in-tray, reminded myself that I had other clients, and settled down to less complicated and more profitable matters.

The grey winter afternoon passed away. Neither Claude nor Alan reported in, but Jayne looked in at closing time to say goodnight and to tell me that Sheila had phoned from a call box in London. The snow was letting up down there and the trains were more or less on time so she was coming home. That cheered me up. I decided to finish the job I was doing, dump the rest back in the in-tray and go home to prepare a warm welcome for my guest.

The square was quiet outside and it must have been about seven when I switched off my dictation machine. Pulling on my overcoat and grabbing my briefcase, I went down the internal stairs to the rear door of the building. After being fire-bombed and broken into last summer I had taken sterner security measures. Now there was an alarm system that could be set from the front or rear doors. I usually set it at the back door, because the lock on the ponderous Victorian front door was clumsy and stuck sometimes.

I punched in the security code and watched the warning light come on. Somewhere above me I heard a phone bleeping, but I couldn't be bothered to answer it. Stepping out through the back door, I pulled it shut, heard the lock click shut and turned around. As I did so I had the sudden vague idea that something was out of order. I wasn't quick enough in tracking down the thought.

With the alarm system I had installed security lamps on the rear of the building. They were triggered by movement or body heat and they should have come on as I stepped out of the door, but I had walked out into a pool of darkness.

Out of the darkness something large and darker lunged at me and I felt a savage blow to the side of my head. I barely managed to keep my footing but I grasped my heavy briefcase and pushed it hard at my attacker. There was a satisfying grunt and whoosh of breath as it made contact, and I took a pace forward. He grabbed the case and tried to wrench it away. I immediately let go and his momentum threw him into a twist, he lost his balance on the sludge underfoot and sprawled full length, cursing.

The yard was walled and almost pitch dark apart from odd glimmers of snow patches. I wasn't about to fight a pitched bout with someone larger than me on that ground – not when he might be armed as Eddie Poxon had been. I was going to kick him hard and then run for the street. I took a pace forward and raised my foot.

That was a mistake, because another shape came at me out of the shadows to my left and something hit me hard across the belly, doubling me up and leaving me gasping. A moment later a heavy blow struck the back of my head and I went right down, collapsing into the trampled sludge. A boot slammed into my face and another into my ribs. I was rapidly losing consciousness when a light flashed and I heard a strange sound. I had another feeling that something was out of order, but this time I never got to work out what it was. Everything went red and then black and I passed out still wondering.

20

I came round in a cubicle at the General Hospital. My head ached furiously, my vision was blurred, there was a pain in my left side and the right side of my face felt like a balloon. Two nurses were working on me, one cleaning up my face and one applying strapping to my ribs. I tried to speak but it came out somewhere between a blurt and a mumble.

As my eyesight began to settle down I realised that I

could see Sheila and Claude peering anxiously over the nurses' shoulders. I tried to grin reassuringly at them but one of the nurses told me not to and anyway I couldn't work my grinning muscles.

The nurses finished their work and covered me up. Sheila and Claude came forward into the cubicle.

'What happened?' we all asked at once, though in my case it came out as 'Wa oppened?'

Sheila clasped my hand and sat beside the trolley. 'I came over from the station,' she said. 'I rang home from the call box and you weren't in, so I rang the office. I guessed you must be just leaving, so I came across.'

'I'd just parked outside,' Claude said. 'When Sheila came along, we saw your light go out, so we walked around the back to meet you and there you were – brawling with a couple of heavies.'

A memory returned. 'What was the noise and the light?' I said. 'Just before I passed out?'

Claude grinned. 'That was Sheila,' he said. 'I flashed my torch, but she pulled out a screamer alarm and went straight in.'

I looked at her admiringly. 'A screamer alarm?' I said.

'Yes,' she said. 'We had a bit of trouble with prowlers on the campus at home, so the Uni shop started selling personal alarms. It seemed like a good idea to get one.'

'It was,' I said. 'But it wasn't a good idea to tangle with those two thugs.'

'Surprise,' she said. 'They thought they'd got you up a dark corner and they could do what they liked. When we came round the corner it shook them, so we had to take advantage of the surprise.'

I shook my head wonderingly, and wished I hadn't. 'Did you get a look at them?'

'Not really,' said Claude. 'Once we came on the scene they were very interested in getting away. I marked one of the bastards and the other one's going to remember Sheila every time he thinks about sex.'

I looked enquiringly at her. 'Nothing much,' she said. 'I just gave him the Adelaide Virgin's One-Step.'

'The police', said Claude, 'are going to be looking for a six-footer doubled over and clutching his crotch, and I took a couple of teeth out of the other one before he got past me.'

I laughed and really wished I hadn't. 'Thanks,' I said, 'both of you. Those sods might have killed me.'

'Somebody's got to look out for you, Chris Tyroll,' she said. 'You're the guy who worried about me being mugged in the Public Records Office and you go wandering about dark yards on your own.'

'The security lamps should have been on,' I said.

'Yes,' she said, 'and you should have used the front door, you galah.'

She bent and kissed me. 'You'll have to do it from the other side,' I said. 'That's the side where they kicked me. I can't feel anything with my lips.'

'OK,' she said, and kissed me from the other side. That one I felt.

A doctor came along and told me the good news. I'd got no serious injuries, only bruising and cracked ribs. He gave me painkillers, warned me about the symptoms of concussion, told me not to jump, laugh or sing for a while and said I could go home. Sheila and Claude packed me into a wheelchair and trundled me out to Claude's car.

Back home they bore me, wincing, to a couch and Sheila departed to the kitchen, muttering about the lengths to which some men would go to avoid cooking a meal. Claude poured himself a large malt and brought me an orange juice.

'Are you interested in how it's going?' he asked.

'If I'm going to get worked over,' I said, 'I might as well know if there's a reason.'

'Well, I haven't found White or the Trumans yet, and Glenys Simpson has left town.'

'I'm told he's still in the licensed trade, but I can't find him yet. He's not in Belston and none of the local landlords know where he is. I've checked the licensing registers at Belston, Wolverhampton, Walsall and Birmingham but he's not listed.'

'So if he's not in Brum he's left the area. He could be anywhere in Britain.'

He nodded. 'Fraid so. Still, there is some good news. I've found Billy Simpson's parents.'

'Good,' I said. 'At least they ought to know something about the relationship between Billy and the lovely Glenys. Maybe they can explain why her conscience didn't hurt her until long after the divorce. But I can't go and see them looking like this.'

Claude grinned. 'Give it a day or two and you'll look even worse. At the moment you've just got a split lip and a great big footprint down the side of your face. Just wait till it all turns green and purple and yellow.'

'Just do me a favour, will you? Give John Parry a ring and let him know what happened.'

The big Welshman arrived in minutes and stayed to drink my whisky and eat my steak while I drank soup and more orange juice. He took statements from all of us and managed not to say, 'I told you so.'

There was a question that bothered me and I asked it.

'Why tonight?' I said.

'What do you mean?'

'I mean that they delivered their threat on Saturday night. It's Monday – how the hell do they know that I haven't written to Mrs Cassidy saying, "Dear Madam, I'm now quite convinced that Alan is innocent but a nasty man from Stoke on Trent has phoned me so your son-in-law can stay in jail for me"?'

'The easiest answer is Claude,' he said. 'They sent their threat – after that they're going to keep tabs on you to see if you're playing ball. They've only got to see you call him in and find out that he's looking for the Trumans and Ben White and they know you're still in play.'

'You mean they're watching me?'

'How else did they know you were alone in the office this evening? You don't just need to keep away from lonely places, you need to keep an eye over your shoulder – and you, Claude.'

21

If 'they', whoever they were, watched me for the next few days they must have got pretty bored. Unable to speak intelligibly to strangers, then unable to speak without wincing, then covered in coloured blotches like a psychedelic panda, I kept to my home. Alasdair called early each morning and we discussed the day's cases in court and any other urgent business. Sheila wanted to abandon her researches and nurse me, but honesty compelled me to admit that it wasn't necessary.

So I spent a lot of time sitting around at home. I tried television, but you have to be sad or mad or both to enjoy daytime TV. It's full of programmes where gloating presenters introduce members of the public whose lives are profoundly and bizarrely dysfunctional and who are delighted by the opportunity to tell millions of housewives about it. I must be getting old, I keep thinking it was better in the old days, when all they showed in the daytime was the test card and colour test programmes.

I could have read books or listened to music or written the book I was always going to write, but I didn't. I sat around and fretted about Walton's case. Nothing fitted, nothing made any sense. I swung backwards and forwards over the facts in my mind and no patterns emerged, no pointers, no explanations that fitted. I got wound up tight over it so that Sheila complained that I talked about nothing else when she came home.

Then Alan Reilly arrived one morning, having emerged from his searches in newspaper files. He had done me proud, bringing me sheaves of photocopies of the coverage of the robbery, the trial of the Trumans and White and the Payday Gang.

The Payday Gang's activities had guaranteed that security van blags were always headline news in the Midland papers and the Belstone Lane job was very big headlines because of the shootings. Happening on a Saturday evening, it gave the press plenty of time to put their stories together before Monday's editions and they filled pages with it.

The front page of Monday's *Express and Star* was decorated with a photo of a fine-featured elderly woman with a commanding look in her eye. The caption said, 'Former POW Daphne Callington, 63, who tried to stop the robbers'.

Daphne Callington meant nothing to me, but the press had made her a heroine. According to them, this disabled sixty-three-year-old had been the only witness to the whole episode and had tried to argue one of the robbers into putting down his gun. I was disposed to believe that the papers had made most of it up, looking for a touch of brightness in the violent horror of what happened in Belstone Lane, but then I read the quotes from Miss Callington:

> 'I was standing at my gate, and he was only a few feet away from me, pointing his wretched gun at the driver. I knew I couldn't get to my phone so I tried to distract him, to delay them until someone else could call the police.'

She had called out to the robber, told him to put the gun down. She had succeeded in distracting him, but the driver had taken advantage of the intervention to try and move. That was when the robber had swung round and loosed both barrels. At the same time someone else's pistol went off. It hadn't been the ruthless, callous slaughter that the judge had called 'an act of evil, conceived in greed and malice'; it had been the kind of stupid cock-up that happens when nervous idiots carry loaded guns.

I looked again at Daphne Callington's photograph. The articles said she had been a mission teacher in her youth, captured by the Japanese at Singapore. She had spent the war in an internment camp. She wasn't making it up and the newspapers hadn't invented her. Why hadn't the prosecutor called her as a witness?

I added another note to my list:

Find Daphne Callington (if she's still alive).

Daphne Callington was interesting, but my next discovery among Alan's photocopies was bizarre. The trial of the Trumans and White had not been widely reported, presumably because they weren't the Payday Gang and they weren't charged with murder, only conspiracy to rob. There had been a few pieces in the press, the kind of pieces that make it nearly impossible to understand what happened in court. You know – a reporter sits in long enough to hear something that will make a headline out of the prosecutor's opening speech. Any barrister worth his wig knows that he's got to say something melodramatic in the first few sentences of his opening. That way he'll get his name in the papers. Then the reporters go away and only come back to hear any witness who they think will make another headline. If there's a conviction, they come in for the sentencing, and the judge says something worth a headline, so he can justify his seven grand a month. When there's an acquittal it often passes unreported.

Piecing together the acquittals of the Trumans and White from that kind of reporting was not easy. The prosecutor had got his opening headline by going as far as he dared to suggest that these were the men responsible for the murder of the Mantons guard, but after that his case fell apart. Policemen's notebooks contained contradictory entries, expert witnesses were not as expert as they seemed and it all went pear-shaped. The Trumans and White walked, with Benjamin White catching a fine for possessing a shotgun without a certificate.

I added another note:

Why were Trumans/White charged?

My old Granny used to say that bad things or good things came in threes. I'd had Miss Callington and the Truman trial; I didn't expect much more, but I turned to the *Birmingham Post* coverage of the Payday Gang trial. There was a lot of it, but it was more thorough than most and it included a complete list of the long indictment that had faced them.

There it was – staring at me in cold print – a charge relating to the Belstone Lane robbery. I shook my head and looked again but I hadn't imagined it. Near the bottom of that long list of charges was one which specified, 'at Belstone Lane, Bellsich, in the Metropolitan Borough of Belston, robbed a vehicle belonging to Mantons of Stoke on Trent . . .'

I groaned. The whole thing was becoming crazier by the minute. *Three* groups of alleged villains had been tried for the robbery! The Payday Gang can't have been convicted, or the charges against Walton and Grady would never have been made.

I read on. The gang had been convicted, after a long trial, of most of the robberies charged, but the jury had been unable to find verdicts in one or two cases and Belstone Lane was one of them. The only evidence presented on that charge was that a sum of money equal to the proceeds of the Belstone job had passed through an Irish bank account days after the robbery and that the account in question was operated by a character called Holland, who had laundered the other robbery proceeds. I imagine the jury decided to give the benefit of the doubt to the Payday Gang on the basis that Holland might have been taking in someone else's dirty money.

It reminded me of something that Malcolm Raikes had said – 'Just remember that I'm not the only antiques dealer in the world and I'm not the only one that the Royals deal with.' Had he meant that the Payday Gang used a number of 'experts' or that other gangs used the same people as the Payday Gang? Or both? Had he been referring to Holland? Or Cook? I groaned again and looked for Raikes' phone number.

'Mr Tyroll!' he exclaimed when we were connected, with the same brightness with which he had greeted me. 'They tell me you've had a little trouble with burglars.'

'It wasn't burglars,' I said. 'It was to do with the Belstone Lane case. And who was the "they" who told you?'

'Oh, you know,' he said. 'One hears these things. What can I do for you today?'

I reminded him of his parting remark when we met. 'There was a man called Holland who laundered money for the Payday Gang,' I said. 'He may have laundered the Belstone Lane cash for somebody else. Is that what you meant?'

'Something like that, Mr Tyroll. Something like that. But I really must go – the doorbell's ringing,' and with that he cut off.

I was still scribbling on large sheets of paper, trying to construct patterns that made sense, an hour later when my doorbell rang. It was Claude and he looked depressed. I insisted on brewing coffee before I heard whatever bad news he brought.

'Some bad news – some good news,' he said, when I asked him what he'd got.

'Go on, then. Bad news first.'

'The bad news', he said, 'is that the Trumans and White have disappeared. Rumour has it that they split for

Manchester or somewhere as soon as their trial was over. Nobody round here has seen them for years.'

'Difficult to blame them,' I said. 'The evidence against them seems to have been really poor. If they were tried for conspiracy to commit a robbery that they didn't commit, especially with a murder at the back of it, you can see why they might not hang about to see what happened next.'

Claude nodded. 'And the good news?' I asked.

'Old pals of the Trumans and Ben White', he said, 'tell me that the late Banjo Cook was a great pal of the Trumans and Ben White. Is that good news?'

'It is – insofar as it's the first piece of information in this bloody case that connects with any other piece. On the other hand, Cook's dead and even the bloke who killed him has vanished, so we're never going to find out what the connection means. My good news is that you can find me an elderly lady called Daphne Callington who used to live in Belstone Lane. I know what her connection with the case is.'

I was wrong about that.

22

I looked in the mirror one morning and discovered that I was only as frightening as usual, so I went back to work. There was a pile of stuff to get through before I could get back on to Walton's appeal, but after a couple of days I'd cleared it.

The next thing I did was write to the Crown Prosecution Service and ask for a copy of any statement made by Miss Daphne Callington. Nowhere in the papers I had could I find a reference to her, let alone a statement. Back when the Belstone Lane case was tried there was no Crown Prosecution Service. The case would have been handled by the

Central Midlands police solicitors and they wouldn't have felt obliged to hand over a statement from a witness they didn't intend using, but even then there was a rule that they should inform the defence of witnesses that they weren't using. It looked as if they hadn't done so, and I couldn't believe that there was no statement taken from Daphne.

Then I sat back and recalled what the solicitor I did my articles with used to say – 'Read every piece of paper and knock on every door. If you don't understand the case then, read every piece of paper again and knock on every door again.' Well, I'd read every piece of paper available to me, so it must be time to knock on some doors.

I started in Belstone Lane, calling on Barrett the insurance man first. He turned out to be a roly-poly, balding bloke with a moustache. He seemed worried at first that I was going to get him involved in something he didn't want to know about, but I explained that I was just going over the ground again for a possible appeal and he simmered down.

We went over his statement to the police and he confirmed that it was correct. He had not been called at the trial; the defence had not argued with any of the evidence that there had been a robbery and murder in Belstone Lane. Then I asked him about Miss Callington.

'Oh, yes,' he said. 'I remember her. She was living next door when we first moved in here. Nice lady – a bit posh and strict, but nice when you got to know her. She had a walking-stick when we first knew her, but then she went on crutches, but she was always trying to do things for people.'

'Do you remember her on the evening of the robbery?' I asked.

'Oh, yes. If it wasn't for her I probably wouldn't have known anything about it till the guns went off, but I heard her shouting at them and that made me look out of the window.'

I looked at his typescript statement again. 'In here,' I said, 'it just says that you heard a woman shout.'

'Yes,' he said. 'In my first statement I said all about hearing Miss Callington shouting at them, but when it was redone the coppers said to leave it out.'

'Did they say why?'

'Yes. They said that Miss Callington was old and disabled and it wasn't right to bother her as a witness and what mattered was what I saw.'

'Who took your first statement?'

'That was the day after – the Sunday. It was two uniformed coppers, a PC and a woman.'

'Then there was this version,' I said, lifting the typescript.

He nodded. 'Yes,' he said. 'That was – oh, I don't know – months later. Two detectives came that time and they had it already typed out. They said it had to be typed out for the court. That's when I asked them about Miss Callington.'

'Miss Callington doesn't live next door now,' I remarked. 'Is she still alive?'

He shook his head. 'I can't say. About a year after the murder she got really bad in the legs and had to have a wheelchair. She had family and they moved her away and the house was sold.'

'You don't know where she went to?' I asked.

He shook his head again. 'Somewhere in the Potteries, I think, but I don't really know.'

'These detectives who brought your second statement, you don't happen to remember their names, do you?'

'It's a long time,' he said. 'I don't know their names. I remember thinking they were a funny pair.'

'Why was that?'

'Well, you weigh people up in my trade, look them over to see whether they've got any money, what's the best approach to make and so on. You can't help it. And you get a certain idea of coppers, from the telly, I suppose, but these two were different. One was a big bloke, all fancy suit, posh haircut, tinted specs – looked too well off for a copper. The other was a squat sort of bloke, thick neck, curly hair, looked quite a nasty bit of work where the other was all smooth and posh.'

I thanked him and left. As I walked down his garden I knew I had found another piece that fitted somewhere. Those two detectives were the late Hawkins and his side-kick, Saffary.

23

I told Claude that Miss Callington had left for the Potteries, and I carried on talking to the witnesses. Pretty boring it was too. All of the Belstone Lane residents had been about their various businesses until they heard the gunshots and the screaming. There was nothing they could tell me that wasn't in their statements to the police.

In three days I knocked on every door in Belstone Lane and talked to all the surviving witnesses. One had died, two had moved away, but there was no reason to believe that they could help me more than the others, so I ended the operation.

I sat at home one night, riffling dully through my notes from Belstone Lane.

'Apart from Miss Callington, there's nothing new at all,' I remarked to Sheila.

'What'd you expect?' she said. 'It was eighteen years ago and, anyway, they didn't see what really happened. They only saw the end. What were you hoping for?'

'I don't know,' I said. 'Better descriptions of the robbers, maybe. Something like that. But by the time they got out of their houses there was blood all over the place and that's mostly what they remember. That and the fact that blokes in masks and dark jackets were running about waving guns, so they ducked inside again and phoned the police.'

'So what next?' she asked.

'Back to Wormwood Scrubs, I think. Now I know the evidence in detail, I'd better talk to Walton again.'

'I'll drive you,' she volunteered.

I looked at her, questioningly. 'It's OK,' she said. 'I've bought a car from a mate of Claude's. After the brawl you got into in your own back yard, I don't like the idea of you trekking about the country on your own.'

Her record for rescuing me from potentially fatal situations was played three, won three, so I didn't argue. Two days later we fought our way through snow and traffic jams into London.

I had carefully armed myself with a letter on Tyrolls letterhead, explaining that I am who I am and signed it, but there was no occasion to present it. The officers on duty were all good manners and efficiency and soon we were sitting in the same yellow-painted room with Alan Walton.

I put names to him – a list of the Payday Gang that I'd culled from the newspapers – Truman, Truman and White. They meant nothing to him. Banjo Cook's name provoked a thoughtful expression.

'Is he black?' he asked.

I nodded. He stared at the wall again. 'And he played the banjo?' he asked, after a pause.

'So I'm told.'

'Yeah,' he said, slowly. 'I saw him once. Billy knew him. Billy used to go around the folk clubs and I think he knew him from there. When the Bowcotts strike was on, there was a fundraiser for the strike at the Black Horse and Billy got this Cook bloke to play at it. What's he got to do with it?'

'I hoped you could tell me. Cook's dead – murdered –

but someone told me that Cook might be someone to talk to.'

He shook his head. 'Don't know anything about him,' he said, 'except that he played the banjo.'

I swore silently. For a moment I had hoped that the mystery of Banjo Cook was about to be revealed, but at least two more pieces had moved slightly closer together – Billy Simpson and Cook had been friends.

I asked him about the Simpsons' home and the intercom between the spare bedroom and the sitting-room.

'Could you tell when it was switched on at the other end?'

He shook his head. 'There was a button on each end that sounded a buzzer at the other end. From Billy's end you had to sound the buzzer and then she'd switch it on and speak. From downstairs you could switch it on without sounding the buzzer, so I suppose she might have listened to us.'

'But she couldn't have heard you planning robberies?'

'No, Mr Tyroll, she bloody couldn't. Because we wasn't planning any.'

'What was their relationship like – Billy and Glenys? She seems to imply that he ordered her about and treated her like a servant.'

He laughed. 'Oh yes! I heard her in court. Proper little mouse she was, all dressed quiet, telling how her husband ordered her about and how she left him because she couldn't take any more.'

'And that wasn't true?'

'I knew Billy all his life, Mr Tyroll. We was at school together. He was the brightest of our lot, a real clever lad. They wanted him to go to grammar school but his parents couldn't afford it. But he was never toffee-nosed about being cleverer than us. He was a really nice bloke with a great sense of humour. When he left school and got a job he used to dress real smart and the girls went for him. He never swanked about it but he could have had any wench in Belston, probably did if the truth was known.'

He drew on his cigarette. 'He had a mouth on him, too. When he was in a good mood he could talk the hind leg off a donkey, charm anyone he could. But he couldn't keep his opinions to himself and he was always losing jobs 'cause he couldn't keep his trap shut about something.'

He smiled reminiscently. 'I worked with him once. We was both machinists at Wharton Engineering in Darlaston. There was a foreman there who was a real pig, treated everyone like dirt and went about like he was cock of the run. They was all afraid of him there and whatever he said the manager'd always back him up. Well, he was a married man, this foreman, but Billy found out as he was having it off with the manager's daughter. I said as he should let the manager know but he said no. He said the manager must know already, that was why he put up with the foreman and always backed him 'cause he day want to upset him and risk it all coming out. Billy says, "What we want to do is make sure everyone knows." And he did. Every time the foreman started picking on someone or playing his face, Billy'd start quietly singing behind his machine.'

'Singing?' I said.

He laughed. 'That's right – singing. He used to sing, "Who's been in bed with the manager's daughter?" and after a bit some of the others'd pick it up and it'd be a sort of chorus. The foreman he'd get furious, but he could never see who was singing, what with them standing behind their machines.'

He laughed again. 'So we had us fun for a few weeks. Then Billy and me got our cards. The foreman said as we hadn't completed our probationary period satisfactorily. Well, that might have been true where I was concerned, but Billy was tops at anything he turned his hand to. He was the best machinist in the place. The others used to ask him if they got into any difficulty.'

He drew on his cigarette. 'I said to him after, I said, "You got us put out of there." He just laughed. He was a bit mad, I reckon, but he'd never let anyone put on him. He was the same when I lost my licence. He said, "I'll get them for you, Alan," and he did.'

'How did he do that?'

'Well, he knew this pub where some coppers drank after hours even when they were on duty. He went there one night with a special camera he had as would take pictures at night without a flash. He got them, all right – three of them coming out the back door and getting into a patrol car. He only sent them pictures to the Chief Constable, dain't he?'

He chuckled. 'Made more trouble for me in the end, though. He sent an anonymous letter with the photos. It said something like, "I see Belston magistrates have disqualified a Mr Walton, a lorry driver. If you're so concerned about drinking and driving, what about this lot coming out of the Bell and Dragon?" '

'How did that make it worse for you?'

'Well, you see I'd built up my little bit of business and you know yourself, in a small business you've got to do most of the work yourself. So I started with just me and a truck, then I got a van and had another driver then I got another truck and a part-time driver. Well, first of all I lost me licence, that was bad enough, but after Billy sent them photos to the police they must have reckoned it was me or a friend of mine did it. They never left us alone. Whenever one of my drivers went on the road, they got stopped. Anything at all they stopped them for – unsafe loads, bald tyres, faulty lights – one of them even got done for not having his number plate vertical!'

He shook his head. 'Well, the lads wouldn't stand for it. They wasn't going to drive for me and get stopped and summonsed all the time, so I couldn't keep anyone and I couldn't drive myself, so I had to pack it in. Still, I never really blamed Billy – he was only trying to do a favour for a mate.'

'And he didn't do you a favour by letting you in on the Belstone Lane job when you were broke?'

'Whose side are you supposed to be on?' he demanded. 'I told you – we was never in any robbery.'

'I'm on your side,' I said, 'but that means I have to test everything. If you weren't in it, was Grady?'

'Do you think he was?'

'In his statement he mentioned a woman shouting at the robbery. Well, I've just discovered that there was one. Where did he get that, if he wasn't there?'

'But that ay his statement, Mr Tyroll – the coppers made it up.'

'And they just happened to make up a woman shouting when there was one?' I said.

'Well, they knew what happened, dain't they? They'd talked to all the people on Belstone Lane, hadn't they?'

I had to admit he was right. 'So Grady really wasn't in it?'

He laughed out loud. 'Grady? Not him! He was all mouth. In the Bowcotts strike the papers started calling him "Red Grady" as if he was some kind of revolutionary. That was a joke. He was a big man in the union all right, when he'd got the others voting for him and backing him, but on his own he was nothing. If I had been doing a robbery I wouldn't have had him with me.'

'What about Hughes?'

He looked thoughtful. 'He was a fairly hard man and he had some tough pals as used his boozer but I don't reckon he'd kill for money.'

'Why wasn't he called at the trial?'

'I wanted him. I wanted him to tell about what happened to him, but my solicitor couldn't find him.'

'He kept a pub. He should have been easy to locate.'

'Ar, but he disappeared, day he? After they let him out he finished with the pub and vanished.'

'You were in a pub on the evening of the murder. Where was Billy Simpson?'

'He was in the pub with us.'

'All evening?'

'Well, no. He come in later.'

'How much later?'

'I don't really recall. It dain't make much odds at the time.'

'So he might have been on the robbery?'

'Give us a break! Billy wasn't that kind. He hated violence. He was a pacifist.'

'He hated banks, didn't he?'

'How d'you mean?'

'Didn't he used to sing a song about the money in banks that belonged to the workers?'

He chuckled. 'So he did, but he wasn't after robbing them. He used to say as we should own the banks and anyway, he was always singing bits of this and that.'

I changed direction. 'You were going to tell me about Billy and Glenys,' I reminded him.

'What's to tell?' he asked. 'I told you – when he was young he was a really smart bloke, and a charmer. Glenys was the same – all the lads was after her and she went through them, one after another. Till she catched up with Billy. She was really set on him. I suppose with his looks and his brains she thought he was going somewhere. He earned good money too. He used to get put out of jobs 'cause of his mouth and his jokes, but there was jobs for the taking then. The bosses day much care why you left your last place if you could do the job.'

He pulled another cigarette from my packet on the table and lit it. 'They got married and she started on him.'

'In what way?'

'Always harping on about money and that. Always wanting more. Well, he give it her at first but she was never satisfied. He reckoned she was going with other blokes. Then they had the kid. He reckoned that'd settle her down. Billy loved that little girl but of course she died, day she. After that there was no holding Glenys. She started treating Billy like dirt and running about everywhere and not taking much trouble to hide it.'

'And it got worse, presumably, when he was out of work?'

'Oh yes. Half the time he day know where she was. We'd go back to Billy's place from the pub and she wouldn't be there. Sometimes she was just going out, all dressed up, as we was coming from the pub. God knows where she went. Belston day have any night-clubs back then.'

'Why didn't she leave him, then?'

'Billy always said as her bloke was married.'

'Did he know who her boyfriend was?'

'He did in the end. He found out. He went out fishing one day, letting on he'd be gone all day. What he did was to wire that microphone thing in their sitting-room on to one of the tape-recorders in his workshop, so as it would switch on if anyone spoke in the sitting-room.'

'So if she brought her boyfriend home, he'd catch them on tape?'

'That's right.'

'Did it work?'

'Oh, yes. He said after that he'd heard him on the tape and he knew who it was.'

'Did he say who it was?'

He shook his head. 'He only said as he was sure of the voice.'

'When was this?'

'Not all that long before we was arrested. Some weeks before.'

'Billy was never arrested though. As I understand it, you three were picked up and Billy committed suicide.'

'We three was picked up, that's right, but Billy day commit suicide.'

'What do you mean?'

'Billy wasn't one to top himself, no matter how bad things were. Someone did for him.'

I was startled. Simpson's death had been one of the few aspects of the case I had accepted at face value.

'What makes you say that? Do you know something about his death?'

'No. Only as he wouldn't have killed himself, no matter what. Someone else did it.'

'Why would that be?'

'I don't know. Maybe it was because of us being arrested or maybe it was because of that wife of his, but he never topped himself. I'm certain sure of that.'

Walking back to the car Sheila asked, 'What next?'

I groaned. 'Try and find out if Simpson really committed suicide, I suppose.'

'You were going to knock on every door,' she said.

'Well?'

'Well, you haven't. When are you going to see Billy Simpson's parents?'

'Soon, I suppose, but I don't want to. Their only son committed suicide – or worse, he may have been killed. All because of their daughter-in-law, and most people think he did himself in to avoid going down for murder and robbery.'

'You've got to do it though, haven't you?' she said.

24

'Do you know,' Sheila said, 'I shall never enjoy a cup of coffee here without thinking about whatsisname and whatchermecallim.'

'Who?' I said.

'You know – the two tramps you said committed murder here.'

'Ah! You mean Moosh and Tiggy.'

We were at Scratchwood Services taking a break on the way home.

'Do you believe him?' Sheila asked.

'What? Walton? What about?'

'About Billy Simpson. Do you believe he was done in?'

'Walton believes it.'

'He would,' she said. 'They were cobbers. Nobody likes to believe that a mate's topped himself. How did he die?'

'He hanged himself.'

'Perhaps he hanged himself the way Banjo Cook did – with a little bit of help.'

'We can't be sure', I pointed out, 'that Cook's death has anything at all to do with it.'

'Don't come the raw prawn with me,' she said. 'John Parry believes it – and so do you.'

'OK. I was just playing devil's advocate.' I sipped my coffee. 'I've never known a case like it. I can't trust anything I read or hear. None of it makes sense and none of it connects.'

'Some of it does,' she said. 'What about Billy Simpson knowing Cook?'

'Right,' I said. 'But did he just know him because he was into folk music? And if there's another connection, what the hell is it? There's no pattern.'

'What sort of pattern do you want?'

'Any sort. Until I find one, I can't begin to make sense. The only pattern I can begin to detect is the presence of Hawkins and Watters and Saffary.'

'They were detectives,' she said. 'You'd expect to come across them in a robbery and murder, wouldn't you?'

'They were bent detectives,' I said, 'and this case is bent all out of shape.'

'Careful,' she warned. 'You don't like Saffary. You'd love to cut him down. Just because you know he's crooked doesn't mean he was crooked here. What did Sherlock

Holmes say about misleading yourself? – "insensibly the theory begins to twist the facts".'

'The facts are already twisted. I'm trying to untangle them. Anyway, why did they tell the insurance bloke not to mention Miss Callington?'

'She was an old lady. She was disabled. Perhaps they thought she'd be a bad witness.'

'Bad witness? She was the only witness they had who actually saw it all from the beginning!'

'OK,' she said. 'Just playing devil's advocate.'

I finished my coffee. 'Take me home to bed,' I said. 'My brain's died.'

'So long as that's all,' she grinned.

Despite Sheila's best efforts I woke in the small hours and lay thinking about Alan Walton's case. Maybe there was a pattern involving Saffary and his unholy chums. My thoughts got scribbled on the bedside pad:

> How did Glenys come to give her information to Saffary & Co?
>
> Why did they deaf Miss Callington as a witness?
>
> Why did they let Hughes go?
>
> Why didn't they arrest Simpson when they arrested the other three? Was Simpson killed? Was he left at large to be killed? If so, why?

All of which brought me back round to:

> Who in the Central Midlands police was prepared to lie to the Court of Appeal to cover something up and what were they covering?

Which was quite enough to put me back into an uneasy sleep.

I had a look at the note in the morning. It looked a bit over the top. It implied that someone in the police had set

Simpson up to be killed and that the force had covered that up.

I bumped into John Parry in the Magistrates' Court and persuaded him to join me in the Rendezvous Café afterwards.

Settled to tea and buttered Chelseas, I told him about my session with Walton and the idea that Simpson was murdered. It didn't seem to disturb him greatly.

'Is that a real possibility?' I asked.

'Anything's possible, bach,' he said, munching steadily. 'But if he was topped the same way that Cook was, then Doc Macintyre would have spotted it. If you want to really upset the old boy, ask him.'

I nodded. Suggesting to the Scots pathologist that he'd overlooked a murder sounded like a recipe for causing another one. Nevertheless, I might have to risk it.

'You agreed with me', I said, 'that the letter to the Court of Appeal clearly meant that the force has got something to hide in this case. Right?'

'Right,' he said. 'Now you're going to ask if I think that someone in the force set Simpson up to be killed and someone else covered it up with that letter. I've told you before, boyo – don't confuse conspiracy with cock-up. Even if – and that's a bloody big if – Simpson was murdered that wasn't the reason for the letter. If Hawkins and his mates killed Simpson, they could hardly go to headquarters and say, "Look, there's a bit of a problem about this Walton appeal, 'cause we stiffed a bloke in that case and we'd be grateful if you'd get it shoved out of court for us." Well, could they?'

'No, I suppose not, but – '

'But nothing! The letter was because someone at HQ knows or strongly suspects that Hawkins and pals were up to their usual tricks, being a bit over-imaginative about confessions and things, and they don't want any more bad publicity. That's all.'

'I suppose you're right,' I said, reluctantly. 'What about them, though?'

'Who?'

'Hawkins and Watters and Saffary. What sort of blokes are they?'

'Hawkins is the dead sort. He was a flash bastard – sharp dresser, loud mouth, always after the women, probably took backhanders, stop at nothing to get a result. Watters is a creepy character – dead eyes, pale face, never raises his voice, always very precise. Underneath it he's a sadist. Saffary you know – thick as a pig, pure Ulster proddy bigot, hates lefties, gays, blacks, Catholics, Jews, Welshmen and you.'

'Why did he hate Simpson, then?'

'Who says he did?'

'Let's just suppose that Simpson was killed and that Hawkins and pals knew about it. There must have been a motive for them to turn a blind eye.'

He stared for a moment. 'Not far to look for a motive with them three – they had motives for being bent coming out of all nine orifices. Hawkins, it'd be women or money or promotion. Watters, it'd be promotion, revenge or the sheer pleasure of nastiness. Saffary, it'd be religion, race, politics, promotion or revenge.'

I chuckled. 'What's funny?' he asked.

'It seems ironic,' I said. 'Billy Simpson was well into revenge. Always believed in getting his own back. He was going to fix Glenys's boyfriend when he died.'

'Then maybe that's it. Perhaps it's got nothing to do with the Mantons job.'

'I thought you once said you didn't believe in coincidence. Get back to revenge, John. Did Simpson ever cross any of Hawkins' team up at all?'

He shook his head. 'Not that I know of, but that means nothing. I've told you, I always tried to keep well upwind of their operations in case the smell stuck to me.'

'Could you find out?'

'Hardly, boyo. Saffary's the only one I see and he doesn't trust me an inch because I eat buttered Chelseas in low cafés with lefty solicitors. Which reminds me that there's just time for you to buy me another.'

I summoned the faithful Ruby with more supplies. Parry's broad face turned thoughtful as he chewed.

'Do you know,' he said, 'if anything, I have a feeling that it was Walton that Saffary had a thing about.'

'Why do you say that?'

'I told you. He and his cronies had a booze-up to celebrate the appeal being thrown out. Saffary seemed particularly pleased that it was Walton.'

'So what did Walton do to him? Apart from hanging about with trade unionists?'

'I don't know, boyo. I don't know.'

Not much result for the price of six Chelseas and four mugs of tea.

25

Sheila had taken a day off from grubbing in libraries and archives and was supposed to be at home, analysing the results, but when I arrived she had the Walton file spread all over my desk.

'That', I said sternly, 'is a confidential file.'

'If you're going to drag me into Wormwood Scrubs by passing me off as your clerk, mate, you can stand back while I do a little clerking. I got bored with transportation records and thought I'd take a squid at Walton's file to see if anything smelt funny.'

'Be my guest,' I said, dropping into a chair. 'But if you stood that file at the end of the garden you could smell it from here. Everything about it stinks.'

She got up and stood behind me, her arms around

my shoulders and her breasts pressed into my back. Her tongue slid into my ear.

'Tea or coffee or whisky or what?' she enquired.

'How about "what"?' I suggested.

'Later,' she said. 'For now it's drinks, then dinner.'

Over a large Talisker I told her about my chat with John Parry.

'Are you going to ask the Doc?' she said.

I nodded. 'I'll have to. Now that Alan Walton has raised the point I've got to check it out. I can't say I relish the prospect, though.'

'Let me do it,' she said. 'Invite him to dinner tomorrow night and let me practise my feminine arts on him.'

That sounded sensible and I agreed. 'What about you?' I asked. 'Was there anything in the file that set off your female intuition?'

She scowled. 'Don't knock intuition, cobber. Sherlock Holmes said that the impression of a woman may be more valuable than the conclusions of an analytical reasoner – so there!'

'I apologise. What would Sherlock have made of the Walton case?'

'He might have shot more cocaine than you're swallowing whisky,' she said, 'but I think he'd agree with me about one thing.'

'What's that?'

'The curious conduct of Desmond Murphy.'

'Who the blazes is Desmond Murphy?'

'He is – or was – the Mantons security manager. There are two very funny things about him. Firstly – he always sent three vans to Belston and varied the pick-up schedules for security reasons. But one of those three vehicles always made the Bellsich pick-up and always passed through Belstone Lane to get there. Isn't that peculiar?'

I nodded. 'So anyone who wanted to rob one of the Mantons vans could easily find out that one of them always passed down Belstone Lane about the same time on Saturday evening. The time would vary a bit, depending on the stops it had made in Belston and traffic and so on, but if someone sat on the Bellsich roundabout for a few Saturday evenings they would be able to work out the time bracket. Not bad, Sherlock. You're not just a pretty face.'

'Say that again and you'll be back in hospital, mate. Seriously, though, it is strange, isn't it?'

'Yes, but the failure of almost all security systems is caused by people getting into lazy, careless habits. Perhaps that's all that Murphy did. He's an ex-copper, isn't he? They're not trained to think logically, you know.'

'Maybe so,' she said, 'but I give you my second point – I draw your attention to the behaviour of Mr Murphy on the evening of the crime.'

'But – let me see – Murphy was out that evening, carrying out routine checking on the Belston vans, right? He waited at Mantons in Belsich for van number 3 to arrive.'

'Right,' she said, 'and when it didn't, what did he do?'

'He went home.'

'Precisely, Watson. He was out checking that everything was apples with the Belston pick-ups according to him. Then one of them goes wrong – goes missing, in fact – and what does he do? He buggers off home, that's what! Logic says that when that van was so late at Bellsich he should have driven back along its route to see whether it had blown a tyre or its crew were in a boozer or what, but he didn't.'

It made a nasty kind of sense and I groaned. 'So maybe it wasn't the Payday Gang, it wasn't the Trumans, it wasn't Billy Simpson and his pals. It was an inside job – is that what you're saying?'

'Not really. It might still have been one of the three favourites, but Murphy may have been in on it. Why don't you send Claude along to put the frighteners on him?'

'He's not going to confess,' I said, 'even to the frightfulness of Claude.'

'Maybe not,' she said, 'but it might stir up some activity.'

'The last time we stirred up some activity, Banjo Cook ended up dead and I ended up in hospital.'

Famous last words.

26

Sheila set up the trap for Doc Macintyre. It wasn't difficult. He lives with a housekeeper even uglier and more curmudgeonly than himself whose cooking he curses daily. An offer of a decent meal would take him anywhere.

She invited my assistant Alasdair to join us. 'He's the excuse,' she explained. 'You're going to discuss Walton's case with Alasdair and Billy Simpson's mysterious death is just going to pop up naturally.'

'Oh, of course,' I said. 'Whereabouts in the menu would you like the late Mr Simpson? With the soup, or later?'

She scowled, fetchingly. 'Just apply yourself to being a good host and helping our guests to enjoy my excellent cooking. After that, you can break out the Talisker and start talking shop but follow my lead, don't blow it and upset the Doc.'

She was evidently well in command, so I confined my activities to fetching and carrying.

Alasdair arrived a little early with a couple of bottles. His taste in wines is good and seems to fit with his expensive, twenties-style suits, his languid drawl and his outmoded upper middle class slang. Only his hand-rolled cigarettes break the pattern. They'd go better with meths or Red Biddy.

'Not knowing what's on the jolly old menu,' he said,

'I brought a bottle of each, red and white. What are we having?'

'Braised kangaroo pouch,' Sheila said straight-faced.

Alasdair plays tennis – of course. He returned the shot effortlessly. 'Top hole!' he exclaimed. 'I've never tried kangaroo, but it's sort of pinkish meat, isn't it? Should go nicely with the Oxford Landing red, that's from down under too.'

Sheila conceded. 'Get him primed,' she ordered, 'before Mac gets here. I'm off to change.'

Minutes later the old pathologist arrived with a bottle of Laphroaig which seemed like a good way of getting us all primed.

When the summons to eat came I was astonished to see Sheila in a dress. She's normally a slacks or jeans person and she hadn't worn a dress since Christmas. Now a cunningly designed red outfit was brightening her ash-blonde hair, making her eyes sparkle and doing quite a lot to display her figure. She was evidently determined to take every kind of advantage of Doc Macintyre and it worked. He was kissing her hand before we reached the table.

Something Indonesian with lots of nuts in it and a dessert created from fruits I didn't know you could buy in Britain put us all in a good mood. Afterwards, in the sitting-room, we broke out the Talisker and Alasdair rolled one of his filthy fags, sucking it into reeking life before taking up his cue.

'How's the Walton case going?' he asked.

'Walton?' said Mac. 'Anything I'm involved in?' He was hoping for an opportunity to regale us with his ghoulish stories.

'Not really,' I said. 'Though you PM'd a bloke called Banjo Cook who was supposed to have hanged himself.'

'Aye, that's right,' he said. 'Murdered, then hung up. Very silly and obvious. Who's Walton?'

Which gave me the perfect excuse to outline the case and my fruitless and confusing enquiries. Mac interjected an occasional question, Alasdair sat silently, sipping his whisky, puffing his cigarette and letting his astonishing memory take hold of the facts.

I told the story more or less chronologically which left Walton's assertions about Billy Simpson's death to the end.

Mac narrowed his eyes across his glass. 'And this Simpson was supposed to have hanged himself?'

'Yes,' I said, nervously.

Sheila moved in swiftly. 'That's pretty unlikely, isn't it, Doc? You said that killing Banjo Cook and hanging him up was silly and obvious.'

'Oh aye,' he said. 'There's a world of difference between hanging a dead body and hanging a live one. No pathologist could miss it. Even a police doctor shouldn't miss it.'

He paused, and I could see a glimmer of suspicion pass across his face. Drunk or sober, Doc Macintyre was still one of the most astute people I knew.

'Did you say that this Billy Simpson was a Belston man?' he demanded.

'Yes,' I said.

'Then he must have been one of my customers,' he said slowly. 'You arenae suggesting that I couldnae tell the difference? Are ye?'

There was a distinct truculence in his manner now.

'Of course not, Mac,' I said. 'That's why I can't believe Walton.'

He subsided, partially mollified, and took a long swallow of whisky. Then he looked up.

'It was a gey while ago, didn't you say? When did Simpson die?'

'About twelve years ago,' I said.

He laughed aloud. 'Well, that buggers your argument, laddie. I wasnae in Belston then!'

The relief around the room could be felt. 'Then who would have PM'd Simpson?' asked Sheila.

'Old Gaythorne and he was a feckless old bugger who just did what the police told him.'

He launched into a tale about his predecessor examining the body of a girl found dead on a piece of waste ground after leaving a party with a man.

'There was evidence of recent sexual intercourse and the coppers were looking for rape and murder, but Gaythorne said it was vagal inhibition.'

'What's that?' asked Sheila.

'It's a rare form of sudden death caused by inhibition of the vagus nerve. It sometimes happens to women who get over-excited in sexual intercourse. It's more common in Scotland than anywhere else.'

We laughed, obediently. He deserved applause after the way we'd tried to set him up.

'I thought you said that Gaythorne did as he was told?' Alasdair said.

'Oh, aye,' Mac said. 'The detective in charge picked Gaythorne up by his lapels – right there, in his own mortuary – and held him up against the wall. "That girl was raped and strangled," he said. "You hear me? She was raped and strangled." '

'And what did Gaythorne do?' I asked.

'He gave evidence against the girl's boyfriend, that's what he did, and the boy got life for murder. Ask John Parry if ye dinna believe me. He was one of the coppers in the case.'

There was silence for minutes. Macintyre broke it. 'So Alan Walton might be right, Chris. If someone wanted to cover up the murder of Billy Simpson, Gaythorne was just the fella to do it.'

'But,' said Alasdair, 'to persuade your predecessor to falsify his report it would have to have been a police cover-up, isn't that right?'

Mac nodded and Alasdair smiled. 'So,' he said, 'you've got a pattern, Chris. The police fail to catch the robbers, then they charge the Truman chappies and fail to convict them, then they lay a charge against the Payday Gang and fail to get a conviction on that, then the lovely and malicious Glenys surfaces and they arrest her husband's pals, but they fail to arrest him and he dies so they can't convict him. Then they let Hughes go without any effort and finally they frame Walton and Grady.'

'And the pattern is . . . ?' I said.

'Deliberate failure, governor. They didn't want to catch the right chappies so they kept going through the motions. Then they put an end to it – with Glenys's assistance – by tidily framing two chaps they didn't like.'

'But why did Glenys have her sudden attack of morality?' I asked.

'Can't say,' he replied. 'I think the coppers set her up to do it. For some reason it was necessary to put an end to the matter, so they used her to knock it on the head. Two chaps in quod for ever – end of Belstone Lane story.'

'And why did Simpson die?' asked Macintyre.

'Because they daren't risk putting him on trial. He must have known something about the real situation. Nor could they risk him being at large when Walton and his chum were tried in case Billy's famous sense of humour and his desire for revenge led him to tell what he knew.'

Around the room heads were nodding thoughtfully. Mine was one of them.

'Then where do we go from here?' I asked.

'Talk to Freddy Hughes. Find Miss Callington. Talk to Sheila's suspect – the security chappy. See what comes up.'

27

It started coming up altogether too fast for me.

We had seen our guests off, chucked the dishes in the

dishwasher and shared a last Talisker while we chuckled over our careful attempts to entrap the wrong pathologist.

'Penny for them?' I said.

'I was thinking about what Mac said about the other bloke – Gaythorne. That terrible story about the boyfriend. I still find it hard to believe that coppers do things like that.'

'It's hard to believe that anyone could do things like that,' I said, 'but you know what Saffary tried to do to me last summer and you know how your grandfather died.'

She nodded. 'Right,' she said. She kicked off her shoes and stood up. 'Come on,' she said. 'Let's to bed.'

'Aren't you afraid?'

'What of?'

'Vagal inhibition.'

'I've told you before, Chris Tyroll – South Australian girls are totally free of inhibition.'

If I'd ever doubted that proposition, she proved it for me again and we collapsed into sleep. For about an hour.

There are many privileges attached to being a solicitor of the Supreme Court in England. Apart from an endless stream of people with problems there are the opportunities to be hassled by the Law Society, the Solicitors' Complaints Bureau and the Legal Aid Board, together with the chance to deal daily with stroppy and unhelpful magistrates, their clerks, court officials, policemen and other lawyers. Then when you get to bed and dream about retirement to the Seychelles, you get woken up in the middle of the night and asked to go to a distant police station and deal with a client who has got himself arrested.

When I dragged myself out of sleep, Sheila was sitting up with a glazed look on her face and the phone in her hand.

'It's Stoke police,' she said. 'They want you.'

I took the phone, wondering dully how the call had come to me. Out of hours calls to my office are diverted automatically to the member of staff delegated to deal with them. That night it was Alan. Any police call to my home must originate with one of the few people who knew my private number.

'Mr Tyroll?' said a voice on the phone.

'Yes.'

'This is Sergeant Mayhew, custody officer at Stoke on Trent police station. We have a client of yours in custody – a Mr Gordon Rains.'

Gordon Rains? Better known as Claude the Phantom! How had Claude got himself nicked?

'I know him,' I said. 'What's the problem?'

'He has been detained at the request of another force, and we are waiting for officers of that force to arrive and interview him. He wishes you to be present at that interview.'

'It's forty miles,' I said, 'and there's snow on the road. I hope you don't want to interview in a hurry.'

'That's all right, sir. The interviewing officers have further to travel.'

'What's this about?' I asked. 'What's he being questioned about?'

'I don't think I can discuss that with you on the phone, sir.'

'And you expect me to drive forty miles in the snow without knowing why?'

'I expect nothing, sir. Mr Rains has asked for you and I have passed on his request. Shall I tell him you won't come?'

Oh, a smart Alec. 'No,' I said. 'I shall be there. In the meantime, can I speak to Mr Rains now?'

'I'm sorry, sir. I've been instructed by my super not to permit that.'

I was still too sluggish to rise to that. I simply told him I'd be there as soon as circumstances allowed and put the phone down.

'It's Claude,' I explained. 'He's been arrested in Stoke on bloody Trent.'

'And you've got to go?' she said.
'I'm afraid so.'
'I'll drive you,' she announced.
'You don't have to.'
'I know that. Get your kit on, while I put some coffee on and fill a flask.'
I thought about arguing. It was quite unjustifiable to expect her to come out in the circumstances. An eighty-mile round trip in vile weather with who knows how long in a police station in between. Then I thought about doing it alone and shut my mouth.
Less than half an hour later we were joining the motorway at Junction 10. The road was covered in a mixture of hard ice and soggy slush and fresh snow was beginning to fall. The only advantage was that no one else was daft enough to be on the road at that time in those conditions.
We made Stoke without any problem. The custody sergeant, as I expected, turned out to be a man in his thirties. The older ones are more polite and helpful.
I introduced myself and Sheila as 'my associate' and asked when and why Claude had been arrested. I am so used to calling him 'Claude' I had to keep forcing myself to refer to him as 'Mr Rains'.
The sergeant consulted the Person in Custody sheet, on the clipboard on his desk.
'Your client was detained at 2200 hours last night,' he said.
Ten o'clock! And it had taken four hours to ring me.
'Why was I not informed earlier?'
'You will be aware', he said (an introduction that is always followed by something pompous and unhelpful), 'that we have discretion in certain cases to deny access to a solicitor.'
'Yes,' I snapped. 'Serious arrestable offences. Are you stating that this is such a case?'
'No,' he admitted. 'But on Mr Rains' arriving here, it became evident to me that there are aspects of the case

that caused me concern, so I referred them to my superintendent. He agreed with me that, initially at least, Mr Rains should have no access to a lawyer.'

'Why has Mr Rains been detained?' I asked.

He looked at me levelly. 'I don't think I'm at liberty to tell you that, yet, other than that he was detained at the request of another force.'

'You have an obligation to provide me with that information,' I said.

'It is, I think, my place to decide on my obligations, sir,' he said.

I shook my head. 'Your obligations – and I remind you that they are personal obligations – are laid down in the Police and Criminal Evidence Act and the Codes of Practice. Please show me the Person in Custody record.'

He looked at me without speaking for a moment, evidently wondering how far he might push it. Then he swivelled the clipboard round on his desk so that I could read the form.

It's a large form on which are recorded all the personal details of an arrested person and it contains an area in which a record of the suspect's detention is supposed to be kept, each entry being timed and signed.

The first entry said:

2218 Arrived at Station in custody of PC 2318 Means and PC 576 Riley. Detained in Greenlow Street when officers observed that

The next two entries read:

2230 Detention authorised to obtain evidence by questioning. Interview will be by Central officers when relevant officers are located.

2232 Details of detention reported to Supt. Lomas who confirmed above actions. PIC denied access to solicitor by Supt. Lomas.

Those entries were signed and the last one counter-signed by Lomas. After five hours at a police station, a suspect is supposed to have his custody reviewed by a superintendent when he is given the opportunity to make any representations or complaints which he wishes. It was now well past the first review time. I looked for the review entry:

0258 Custody reviewed. Further detention authorised to await arrival of Central officers for interview.

That was in the handwriting of and signed by Lomas.

I copied the entries into my notebook and swung the clipboard back.

'This record is incomplete and not in compliance with the Act,' I said. 'No reason for his arrest is recorded nor any reason for denying him a solicitor.'

'With respect, Mr Tyroll,' he began (another introduction which presages unhelpful sarcasm), 'the reason for his detention is sensitive. Furthermore, when detained he explained his presence in this city by reference to enquiries which he was carrying out for you. It was felt that, when he asked for you to attend, there might well be a conflict of interest on your part. A large part of the delay in contacting you was caused by Mr Rains' refusal to accept the services of the duty solicitor.'

'Sergeant,' I said, 'the Act requires you to record the reason for arrest in all cases, regardless of sensitivity. As to conflict of interest, that is a matter for me to decide and for the Law Society or the Solicitors' Complaints Bureau to take up if I am wrong. Is Superintendent Lomas still on duty?'

'Yes, sir.'

'Please let me see him, immediately.'

Without further word he picked up the phone and punched out a number. As he made his call he kept a wary eye on us, as though he expected us to pinch the ballpens from his desk.

'Superintendent Lomas will see you shortly,' he said and waved us to a bench.

Five minutes later the door opened and the superintendent appeared. He was a short, plump man with a rosy complexion and a neatly clipped moustache as white as his hair and his uniform shirt.

He led us up to the first floor and showed us into his office. When we were seated he rubbed his hands, nervously I thought, and smiled.

'A filthy night to be called out,' he said. 'Can I get you tea or coffee?'

When a policeman you don't know offers you tea or coffee, it usually means they've got something to hide, but we accepted and he ordered by phone.

Turning from the phone he rubbed his pink hands again.

'I understand you're here about Mr Rains,' he said, as if there was some doubt.

'Yes,' I said. 'And your sergeant, who refused to tell me on the phone why my client has been arrested, has now refused that information again. In addition to which, the Person in Custody Record has been improperly left incomplete. May I now ask why Mr Rains is in custody and what is so sensitive about the matter that you have permitted a blatant breach of the Police and Criminal Evidence Act?' I said it evenly, but I was furious.

He lifted both pink, well-manicured hands. 'Now, don't let's get off on the wrong foot, Mr Tyroll. Firstly, Mr Rains was detained by officers on mobile patrol in Greenlow Street at about ten o'clock.'

'Where and what is Greenlow Street and why was he detained?'

'It's a residential street, quite good class, and the officers were routinely patrolling when they spotted Mr Rains' car. They detained him because the registration number of his car was on their orders as a vehicle to be looked out for and its driver detained.'

'For what reason?'

He shifted uncomfortably in his chair. He was rescued by a constable arriving with the coffee. He made a great performance with the sugar sachets, then asked, 'Where were we?'

'We were wondering why Mr Rains was detained.'

'Ah, yes. Well, there is a little difficulty there. The reason for his detention is sensitive.' He paused.

'So am I, Mr Lomas. If I hear the word sensitive again, I shall scream.'

He stared unhappily across my head, as though the answer to his problem was written on the wall. Then he seemed to come to a decision. He hunched forward and clasped his hands on his blotter.

'You are familiar with the work of the Special Branch?' he asked, dropping his voice as though there was a spy at the keyhole.

I nodded. The Special Branch are Britain's political police. They do the legwork in this country for the government's intelligence agencies. They also deal with immigration matters and anything that smells of politics. What the hell had Claude got himself into?

'Well, the Branch keeps its activities very secret – quite properly, of course – but they do call on us ordinary coppers for assistance in certain ways.'

I nodded again and he seemed pleased.

'From time to time we receive from the Branch lists of vehicles that interest them. Normally the request is merely to observe and report those vehicles if they are seen on our patch. Occasionally we are asked to detain the driver. Mr Rains was detained as the result of such a request from the Central Special Branch.'

He sat back, as though he had explained everything.

'For what offence?' I asked.

'I don't know,' he replied, looking quite surprised.

'Superintendent Lomas,' I said, 'you must know that there are only two justifications for an arrest – either the possession of a valid warrant to arrest or reasonable suspicion that an arrestable offence has been committed. You seem to have neither.'

He spread his hands again. 'I feel that the Special Branch request provides me and my officers with reasonable suspicion,' he said.

'With reasonable suspicion of what, Mr Lomas? Mr Rains was entitled to be told the reason for his arrest. He cannot have been. He has been falsely arrested and wrongfully imprisoned. Please release him – immediately.'

'Now be reasonable, Mr Tyroll. I have to act on the lawful request of another force, which I have done. Now, when we first contacted Central after Mr Rains was brought here, they said they'd send officers, but they haven't done so. I have phoned them again and they seem to be uncertain as to who issued the request to us in the first place. Now, as you have pointed out, that puts me in a difficult situation so I have faxed Central asking for clear further instructions immediately, failing which I shall have no option but to admit Mr Rains to bail.'

He finished this announcement with a triumphant smile, as though he were the only man who was doing the right thing.

'You cannot', I said, 'admit Mr Rains to bail without his consent, which I can assure you you will not get, and you cannot hold him without reasonable suspicion which you have not got. If he is released immediately I shall merely advise him to sue the Chief Constable. If you delay, I shall advise him to sue you, your sergeant downstairs, and PCs Means and Riley.'

'He can, if he wishes, sue the Chief Constable, of course,' he replied stiffly.

'And you and your subordinates personally, Superintendent. Now – are you going to release him?'

'Suppose I allow you to see him and explain the situation, while I try to get a clear answer from Central?' he said.

I stood up and looked at my watch. 'I'll give you thirty minutes,' I said. 'After that I shall deem it necessary to wake a judge in the middle of the night and apply for a writ of habeas corpus.'

He picked up the phone and told the custody sergeant we were on our way and were to be allowed to see Claude.

Claude was sitting in a small cell, feet up on the bench, looking entirely at ease with the world and as crisp as usual.

'What happened?' I asked.

'Well,' he said, 'I'd been on the track of your Miss Callington. I found out that, when she left Belstone Lane, she came to live with relatives up here and I finally tracked them down. Now they were a bit suspicious at first, but eventually they told me that she's still alive, still *compos mentis*, but she's bedridden and permanently resident in a nursing home near Stafford.'

'Great,' I said, 'Well done. But how did that get you arrested on a tip-off from the SB?'

He looked bewildered. 'The Special Branch? Still, I suppose that's right.'

'Why? What have you been up to?'

'Well, the arresting officers just said that they had orders to arrest me.'

I nodded. 'That seems to be true, and those orders came from Central Midland's Special Branch.'

'When I got here, the superintendent implied, without stating it, that it was a terrorist enquiry.'

'If it was a Prevention of Terrorism Act arrest, they'd have kept you incommunicado,' I said. 'That's a guaranteed reason.'

'Right,' he said. 'But he didn't say it was a PTA arrest. He managed to suggest that it was an enquiry from Interpol.'

'Interpol! This gets more bloody bizarre every minute.'

The cell door rattled and the custody sergeant appeared

with Lomas at his back. The superintendent almost swaggered into the cell, thumbs tucked under the pocket-flaps of his shirt.

'Well now, Mr Rains,' he said, affably. 'You will be pleased to know that I've sorted it all out with Central Midlands. They'd got it all wrong somehow. It wasn't you they wanted at all, so you can go your way. May I say how sorry I am that you've been inconvenienced? If you have any complaints about your treatment while in our custody I shall be pleased to hear them.'

Claude's normally impassive face was a picture. He swung his legs off the bench and stood up so that he towered over the portly superintendent in the close confines of the cell.

'The only complaints I have', he said, 'are that I was arrested without a valid reason, unlawfully confined in a cell and denied access to my solicitor for hours and I have no doubt Mr Tyroll has already expressed his views on that.'

Lomas became brusque. 'Then we'd better return your property and see you out,' he said, leading the way out of the cell.

28

We left Claude at the desk, recovering his property and signing to certify that Sergeant Mayhew hadn't stolen his small change. Outside we saw that there was no fresh snow on the car's roof. With luck, we might be home before the next fall.

As we pulled out of the police station car-park Sheila switched on the windscreen wipers, then cursed loudly. Both wipers were bent at odd angles and rattled uselessly against the glass. She pulled to the roadside.

'Look at that!' she exclaimed. 'Vandalised in a police station car-park, while the guardians of law and order are arresting the innocent! I've a good mind to go back in there and tell Superintendent bloody Lomas just what I think of him!'

'Don't do that!'

'Why not?'

'Because he will stop us travelling in an unsafe vehicle and we'll be stuck here until we can get a cab to make a forty-mile trip in the snow.'

'We could get Claude to give us a lift.'

'It'll take him too far out of his way. We'll just have to make the best of it and hope it doesn't snow again.'

We broke out the coffee flask, woke ourselves up as far as we could and headed south along streets as empty as when we came. Soon we were on the motorway, splashing through the brown slush that spread all over the middle lane. Earlier motorists seemed to have stuck to that lane keeping it partly clear, but either side of us were stretches of ice with fresh snow on top and edges of packed frozen slush that banged against our wheels when the slush caused slight skids. I trusted Sheila's driving but I would be a lot happier when we were back in Belston.

Several miles south of Stoke Sheila remarked on headlights behind us. 'Must be Claude,' I said. 'He should overtake us. That thing of his is a lot heavier than us. He shouldn't be sliding the way we are.'

The lights drew closer but fell in behind some distance back. I assumed that someone was keeping a safe distance and got back to worrying about Claude's arrest. We had known for some time that he was being watched, but this was different. It was unlikely that the Central message had gone only to Staffordshire. Maybe he was now at risk wherever he pursued enquiries, and perhaps that was the point of the exercise.

I had given up and was fast succumbing to tiredness when Sheila spoke.

'Here he comes,' she remarked.

The following car had speeded up and moved into the outside lane, apparently to overtake. As I turned to look, I realised that there was a passenger in it.

'It's not Claude,' I said. Then some instinct flickered in my tired brain. 'Be careful!' I warned.

They drew alongside and, instead of forging ahead, stayed beside us. Sheila gave them a quick glance – all she could afford on that road – and slowed slightly. They dropped back to match us and I saw their passenger window slide down.

Sheila needed all her attention to keep us in lane, but I could not take my eyes off the passenger in the other car. I saw him bend his head and reach for something at his feet, then straighten up. I fully expected a gun and I was tensed to pull Sheila down in her seat.

As the passenger raised something to the window I caught a glimpse of it and thought that I was hallucinating. For a split second it crossed my mind that I had dozed off and dreamt the whole episode. He was holding a large, brightly coloured, kids' pump-gun.

My mind couldn't take in the combination of deadly threat and the ludicrous toy gun in the split second that followed – before he fired his bizarre weapon and a thick jet of brown, icy sludge poured out across our windscreen.

Instinct tells you to brake when you can't see, and Sheila started, but only for a second before sense told her not to brake hard on the sludge beneath us. We had begun to slide at the rear as she started to brake, but now she swung the wheel hard, aiming into the inner lane.

There was a savage bang and the car lurched as the front wheels hit the barrier of frozen sludge between the lanes and crushed across it. For a brief moment we were under control and making into the inner track, then the bite of our wheels on the fresh snow slowed the front, allowing the rear, still in the slimy middle lane, to swing vigorously. We went into a series of circular skids, spinning helplessly down the road, battering back and forwards across the ice barriers and lurching up and down. From the side and rear windows we caught glimpses of the road going round and round us. We could not see our attackers.

The blinded nightmare seemed to go on interminably while Sheila fought the wheel and cursed fluently, then we skated to a stop and hit something hard with our nose. Instantly we unbuckled our seat belts and piled out.

We had come to rest on the hard shoulder, slewed in at an angle with the front end crushed against the base of a direction sign. I looked around. Fifty yards ahead of us, another car was parked on the shoulder and two dark figures were walking towards us. I grabbed Sheila and pulled her down behind the car.

'What now?' she said.

'Now they finish us off,' I said. 'They won't shoot. This has to be an explicable accident, hence the sludge trick.'

I looked round again, desperately seeking cover or support. The road was empty in both directions and I recalled that our attackers were the only vehicle we had seen since setting out. Then a pair of lights topped a slight rise behind us. The men walking towards us stopped, conferred, and headed back to their car.

As they drove off Sheila reached into our car. 'Want a coffee?' she asked, lifting the flask out of the interior.

Moments later Claude the Phantom drew up alongside us. 'Got another cup of that coffee?' he said. 'That police station stuff is vile.'

29

You may walk away from an incident like that, but it frightens the hell out of you and stresses you like mad, so you can imagine that we took the next day pretty easy, rising late and staying at home. By the afternoon I had recovered from tiredness and fright sufficiently to get my mind back on the case.

I rang the nursing home where Miss Callington lived, to make an appointment for the next day. I had some experience of the vulnerability of old people in nursing homes and I wanted to get to her before someone else did. Her family had told Claude that she was of sound mind, but I checked with the home's Matron.

She laughed. 'Miss Callington', she said, 'is a good deal sounder of mind than most of us, Mr Tyroll, never fear!'

Moments later Claude rang. 'Struck lucky,' he reported. 'Hughes wasn't on any licensing register in the conurbation but I've got him. He's in Shropshire – still in the trade.'

Sheila and I took a cab out early that evening. Hughes' pub was in a back street of a small market town, well west of his former haunts, an old, unpretentious building that no brewer had thought worthwhile tarting up and renaming. Inside it was cosy, bright and warm, with open fires in its small rooms.

Hughes, a thickset, balding man with a round, pink face, was serving at his own bar. When I introduced us he lifted the flap and led us through into a small private parlour.

'I wondered when you'd get round to me,' he said, as we sat and he brought us drinks.

'You expected us?' I said.

He grinned. 'I had that Saffary round here, just before the lads appealed.'

'What did he want?'

He swallowed a large gulp of mild. 'Just to tell me to keep my mouth shut if anyone asked me about the case.'

'To keep your mouth shut about what?' I asked.

He grinned again. 'I don't know. I never knew anything about the bloody case any road. He came back again after.'

'What was that for?'

'To say as you was looking into it – "muckraking" he said – and to remind me to say nowt.'

'And is that what you're going to do?'

'I can't tell you anything about the robbery and the shooting,' he said, 'for a very simple reason – because we warn't involved. Not me, nor Alan nor Peter.'

'What about Billy?'

He looked at me silently for a moment. 'Ah, well,' he said, 'I always thought as he might have been.'

The same thought had occurred to me more than once. 'Why do you think that?'

He drank again. 'He was a funny bloke, Billy Simpson. A lot smarter than the average and he had some funny friends.'

'Like Banjo Cook?' I hazarded.

He nodded. 'You know about Cook?' he said.

'Only that he and Billy were pals.'

'Oh, they was good mates,' he said, 'and they was alike in some ways. Both smart buggers, both with no money to speak of, but neither of them went short. Of course, all Billy's cash went to that bloody Glenys but Banjo used to spend like there was no end.'

'What did he do?'

'Do? He played the banjo, that's what, and he didn't make the kind of money he had playing the bloody banjo.'

'Where do you reckon it came from?'

'He used to knock about with the Trumans and Whitey – they called him that 'cause he was blacker than the rest of them. You know, the ones that got away with the robbery?'

'Do you think they did it?'

'Possibly. I heard as Banjo put them into it, then he took the lion's share of the loot and when they started playing their faces about it he shopped them.'

'Is that why he was killed?'

He shook his head firmly. 'No – if that story's right he had the coppers on his side. The Trumans wouldn't dare touch him.'

'So who killed him?'

He grinned again. 'You know, don't you? I heard tell as you was there.'

'I know who did it, but I don't know why.'

'Might have been lots of folks – I told you, Banjo made his money some funny ways.'

All of this might be good stuff or it might be totally misleading, but I was having trouble taking it all in and keeping abreast of our conversation. I thought for a moment.

'You say that Billy might have been involved and that Banjo Cook might have got the Trumans and White involved. If they did it, what's Billy Simpson's connection?'

'He was a planner, warn't he? A scout and a planner.'

'A planner? Who for?'

'Mainly the Payday Gang, warn't it? He was unemployed, he used to look out for jobs for them and set them up with a plan. He dain't take part, but he got his cut.'

'You're sure of this?'

'Billy and me went back a long time. He told me, didn't he?'

'But if he was a planner for the Payday Gang, how come the Trumans did Belstone Lane?'

'I don't know,' he said. 'Maybe the Payday lot didn't want it or perhaps they didn't reckon it. It was a bit small compared to some of their'n.'

'And you were never involved in any of Billy's plans?'

'Mr Tyroll,' he said, 'I don't mind talking about Billy's business – he's dead. I don't mind talking about Alan and Peter's business – they sent you. But I ain't talking about my business, right?'

It was said in a friendly enough tone. It not only laid down the boundaries – it added a considerable amount of credibility to his evidence.

'But you weren't in the Belstone Lane job.'

'No. No way.'

'And when you got arrested, what happened? After all, you say that Alan and Peter weren't, but they stuck a fake confession on one and used it to convict both of them. How'd you walk out?'

He laughed. 'They went at us, all three of them, Hawkins, Watters and Saffary, and they'd keep going from one to another of us, trying to get one of us to grass up the others, but it dain't work. Even when they showed me Peter's so-called confession, I wouldn't admit anything because there wasn't nothing to admit.'

'Peter Grady never implicated you in his statement.'

'He did in the one they showed me,' he said. 'I still wouldn't give them anything, so they wrote out one for me, just like they must have done with Peter.'

'What then?'

'Saffary stuck it on the table and said, "Sign that, or we'll have you here for ever." '

'What did you do?'

'Well, I was pretty sick of being locked up and shouted at by them, so I thought I'd bring things to a head. I took the statement and you know the thing as you have to write at the bottom – the bit that says it's all true?'

'The caption? Yes.'

'Well, I started to copy that off of the card they showed me, but I made it different. I wrote, "This statement is not true and I have not made it of my own free will, I have signed it because Hawkins and Watters and Saffary threatened me." '

It was my turn and Sheila's to laugh. 'What the blazes happened?'

'Well, they didn't catch on at first. They thought as I was writing their words off of the card, but then Hawkins saw what it was and he clouted me, right in the face. Then he picked up the papers and he tore them in pieces. Then they all went out and left me.'

He paused and drank, enjoying the recollection, as he had every right to do.

'About half an hour after, Saffary came back. He unlocked the cell and just said, "Get out!" I said, "What's this?" and he said, "You can go." I said, "I thought you was going to keep me here till I confessed everything." He said, "Another time'll do for you. I want that bastard Walton." And that was it. They let me go.'

'Did anyone ever say why Saffary had a down on Walton?'

'Not that I ever heard, but Saffary hated him.'

He had made a lot of things clearer. I thanked him and we had a quick short with him before leaving. As he showed us out he said, 'Get them out if you can, Mr Tyroll. They're good lads and they dain't do it.'

It reminded me of Mrs Cassidy and Tracy.

30

Miss Callington's nursing home was in a village a few miles from Stoke. Sheila was all for hiring a car, but I was happier travelling by train. Nobody's ambushed one of those in Britain since before I was born.

Before we left it occurred to me that Desmond Murphy, the former Mantons security manager, might live somewhere in the area if he was still alive and it might be possible to kill two birds with one stone. Alasdair Thayne is our office computer nut, i.e. the only one around who both uses and understands them. I knew he had a program that would search for the phone number of anyone listed in the UK. I asked him to try 'D. Murphy' in the Stoke area and he had three in minutes.

I switched on a tape to save taking notes, and started

dialling. My luck was in. On the first call a testy, flat Potteries voice snapped, 'Murphy! Who is this?'

I introduced myself and asked if he was the former Mantons man. 'I was, yes,' he said, 'but I don't see how I can help you. Anything I knew I told to the police at the time. You must have a copy of the statement I made to Gerry Hawkins' lads.'

'I believe you're a former police officer yourself?' I said.

'I am,' he said. 'Staffordshire, then Central Midlands, so I knew what they wanted and I gave it to them. That was years ago, I can't tell you any more now.'

'There was really only one thing,' I said. 'It was in your statement, but I didn't really understand it.'

'What was that?' he said.

'You were out that evening making procedure checks on your van crews in the Belston area.'

'Yes.'

'And, according to pattern, the third van would come through Belstone Lane to Bellsich High Street?'

'Yes.'

'You said that you waited, was it half an hour, at Bellsich but they didn't show up?'

'That's right.'

'Did it occur to you to drive down Belstone Lane and see what had kept them?'

'Listen,' he said. 'I never got paid for those evening checks. I just did them because I thought they needed doing and I wasn't there to wetnurse them if they'd had a flat or something. When they didn't show up I marked them down for a talking to on Monday and I went home. That's all.'

'Thank you,' I said. 'That's all I needed to know.'

He put the phone down without a word. I stopped the tape, dropped the cassette into my briefcase and Sheila and I headed for the train.

On the way north we discussed the previous night's interview with Hughes.

'Is he telling the truth?' she asked.

'What's he got to lie about?'

'To get his cobbers out of jail?'

I shook my head. 'If he was trying to do that, he'd have been more directly helpful.'

'Was he helpful?'

'I think so,' I said. 'I believe I've got a better idea of what may have happened.'

'Like what?'

'Suppose Billy Simpson put the Mantons job up to the Payday Gang and they turned it down. So, he offered it elsewhere – like to Banjo Cook?'

'That's what your antiques dealer meant, isn't it? The Payday Gang had more than one planner and Billy Simpson scouted for more than one gang.'

'Brilliant!' I said. 'That's got to be right. So he gives it to Banjo Cook who gets the Trumans and White involved.'

'You think they did it?'

'Hughes thinks so and he seems to know. Just go with my theory a moment. They do the job but after the killing they're scared. Cook holds on to the loot. They turn nasty on him . . .'

'. . . and he dobs them in,' she finished. 'But why don't they get convicted?'

'If Alasdair's right, because somebody doesn't want them to be.'

She frowned. 'But who? Banjo Cook doesn't mind them going down – he's got the loot and they obviously couldn't tie him to the robbery. So who else didn't want them convicted?'

'Maybe John Parry's right. Perhaps we're thinking conspiracy when it was just cock-up but the effect is the same. The police still have an unsolved murder, so when Glenys comes along they're delighted. They can convict someone who Saffary has some kind of grudge against and claim the credit. And they didn't pull Simpson in because he just might have told the truth. How's that?'

'Why'd they let Hughes go so easy?'

'They only needed him to convict Walton. Once Grady signed a statement they knew they'd got Grady and Walton. They didn't need Hughes.'

'There were four robbers. Why would they settle for two?'

'They weren't settling for two. Everyone on that jury knew that Simpson had committed suicide. They settled for three out of four and used Grady's statement to make it look as if they'd nailed the important ones.'

'That's another thing,' she said. 'Why were there two versions of Grady's statement?'

'One without Hughes if he co-operated – one with him if he didn't.'

She nodded slowly but the nod turned to a shake. 'It won't work,' she said.

'Why not?'

'Because you've tied it all up neatly between Billy Simpson and the Payday Gang and the Trumans. That leaves a lot out.'

'Like what?'

'Like who killed Billy Simpson?'

'We can't be sure he was killed.'

'Lawyer's bullshit, Chris Tyroll! And even if he wasn't, who had Cook killed? And why are the police covering up? And who had you beaten up? And who tried to kill us on the road?'

I raised my hands in surrender. 'OK! OK! It was just a theory. Have you got a better one?'

She shook her head again. 'Only an outline,' she said. 'Saffary was happy to convict Walton because he's got a down on him and anyway, they needed a conviction. They cut corners to do it, so the force is covering up. But somebody may have killed Billy Simpson and somebody did have Banjo Cook iced and somebody's been after you twice and had Claude watched.'

She stopped and I waited, but that seemed to be it.

'Are you saying you know who's behind all that?'

'After Stoke on Trent we know damned well who had Claude watched.'

'Are you saying the police did it – had Simpson and Cook killed?'

'Who else? When you have exhausted the impossible, whatever remains, however improbable . . .'

'. . . must be the truth. Stop quoting Sherlock Holmes at me. You really think the fuzz did it? You must have some awfully nasty coppers in Aussie!'

'You've got some awfully nasty coppers in England and you'd do well to remember it!'

'But why?'

'That', she said, 'is the bit I can't work out.'

31

Miss Callington had put on her best bedjacket for us. Considering her disabilities and the passage of time, she looked remarkably like her photo in the papers at the time of the robbery. Her large nose was still surmounted by a pair of eyes sharper than many younger ones and, despite being bedridden, her head had an imperious lift.

She welcomed us into a warm, spotless room with attractive and colourful prints on the walls. A window looked over a garden that must be very pretty when not blanketed in snow.

She seized on Sheila's accent as we introduced ourselves. 'You're a long way from home, my dear. What does a South Australian girl make of an English winter?'

Sheila laughed. 'Hard going,' she said. 'I've been in

Britain several times, but never in winter before. You've been in South Australia?'

'I was a mission teacher before the war, and before the Japanese did this to me,' and she gestured towards her legs, 'I worked among the aborigines. Have you ever heard of Daisy Bates?'

Sheila nodded. 'I'm a social historian by trade,' she said. 'I've read up a lot on Daisy Bates.'

'Then you know about her camp at Ooldea. I used to go up there on the Transcontinental Railway. They used to call the train the Tea and Sugar because that's what it brought them.'

A tap at the door heralded a girl with a tea-tray. She placed the tray on a bed-table and pushed the table across Miss Callington's bed.

'You must let me be mother,' the old lady said. 'There are very few things left that I can do, but I can still pour an honest cup of tea,' and she did so with as steady a hand as I have seen.

'Now,' she said, 'what brings an Australian social historian to Britain? You're not studying us, are you?'

'As a matter of fact, yes. I'm working on a study of the families from which the convicts came. Trying to track them down, particularly the descendants of the few who came back.'

'How fascinating! You must let me read it, my dear. Don't be too long about writing it, though!' and she laughed heartily.

'Now, Mr Tyroll,' she went on. 'Here we are chattering away and you're on business. You told the Matron that you wanted to talk about the Belstone Lane murder and you asked her if I was still *compos mentis*, did you not?'

I blushed. 'I did, I'm ashamed to say, but I now see that the question was unnecessary.'

'Well, I can certainly recall what happened in Belstone Lane,' she said. 'For months afterwards I had dreams about it. I saw a lot of dreadful things done by the Japanese, but what happened to those poor men from Mantons was different. One does not expect to be confronted by violence and bloodshed while one is budding one's roses.'

She fell silent and fingered the spectacles that hung from a chain round her neck.

'And I thought, perhaps, that I had caused it, you know,' she went on. 'If I had not distracted the man with the shotgun the driver would not have been encouraged to try and get away.'

'It can't have been your fault, Miss Callington,' said Sheila.

The old lady nodded slowly. 'I realised that, in the end. I came to see that, if foolish and cowardly men go about their illegal business with guns, they will end up killing someone sooner or later.'

'Miss Callington,' I said, 'I believe you made a witness statement at the time?'

She nodded. 'That's right. The next day.'

'Do you recall the officers who took it?'

'There was a squat coarse-featured man with a Northern Irish accent and another man with greasy black hair and unpleasant hooded eyes.'

'Saffary and Watters,' I said for she had described them exactly.

'That may have been their names,' she said. 'Do you have a copy of my statement?'

'No, Miss Callington. It was not among the papers supplied to me. I have written to the Crown Prosecution Service, but they have not replied. I have read what you told the local papers but I shall be grateful if you can tell us what you remember about the incident and I shall be glad if you will let me record your remarks.'

I took a cassette recorder from my case, switched it on and stood it on the table.

In a clear, strong voice she recalled that evening, eighteen years before. She told us how she had made her way on two walking-sticks to her front gate to bud her best rose bush. Leaning on the gate she saw the Mantons van and watched it trapped between the car and the van that carried the four robbers. The robbers had all been armed, two shotguns and two pistols, but once the driver and his mate had been threatened out of the van, two of the attackers had busied themselves unloading cash bags into their van and car. The other two, one with a pistol and one with a shotgun, kept the van's crew at gunpoint.

There had been no one in the neighbouring gardens and she knew she could not get to her phone quickly, and so she decided to try and distract the robbers until a neighbour noticed what was happening and called the police. Her distraction was marvellous and typical of this spirited lady – she simply ordered the nearest villain to drop his gun. He had swung the gun upon her and she might have been the victim of his nervous fingers, but while she exchanged opinions with him the Mantons driver had started to edge towards the robber. Catching sight of the movement the robber swung, the shotgun exploded in his nervous fingers and his colleague, equally nervous, fired his pistol.

The driver's mate had died instantly from a single pistol shot. The driver received both barrels of the shotgun and lived to be legless. Miss Callington had clung to her gate, sickened, as the robbers, screaming blame at each other, bundled the last of the cash in their vehicles and took off in opposite directions. One of Miss Callington's neighbours had seen the shootings from her upstairs window and became hysterical.

She finished her recital, which had been cool and precise throughout, and looked at me.

'Is that what you required, Mr Tyroll?'

'Admirable,' I said and I meant it. This was the witness the Crown did not call and she remembered it all still. She had never once stated a fact of which she was not sure and had been quite clear when she was offering an opinion and not a certainty. She would have been a dream witness and any barrister who tried to cross-examine her would have sunk without trace – but they had not called her.

She had described the robbers as all dressed alike in dark jackets, ski masks and gloves, but her recall was so good I decided to try a long shot.

'I know they were masked, Miss Callington, but might you be able to recognise any of them – the man with the shotgun, for instance?'

'I very much doubt it,' she said. 'Even the man with the shotgun, who was only three yards from me, was only eyes and patches of skin behind that absurd mask.'

I took out a photograph of Alan Walton at the time and passed it to her. She picked up her spectacles, put them on and laughed aloud.

'Oh no, Mr Tyroll!' she said. 'I can't have made myself clear. The man with the shotgun was a black man, and I am reasonably sure that the others were.'

Now I knew why she hadn't been called at the Payday Gang trial, because they were all white and the same applied to Walton and Grady. But why hadn't they called her at the trial of the Trumans?

'You're sure?' I pressed. 'After all, you did see only patches of skin and eyes.'

'It was the language, more than anything. He shouted at me – filth, obscenities. Then when the guns had gone off, they all shouted at each other.'

'You understand West Indian obscenities?' I asked, astonished.

She looked at me severely across the top of her spectacles. 'Young man,' she said, 'I was a mission teacher. I have been roundly abused by every kind of Briton, by Australians, Dutch, Japanese, most varieties of Asians and Africans and by West Indians. I knew exactly what he said to me and what they said to each other.'

I should have remembered my thoughts about anyone who tried to cross-examine her.

I had only one more point. 'Miss Callington,' I said, 'did

anyone ever suggest that you might be called as a witness at the robbers' trial?'

She shook her head. 'I recall that the police said that no one was arguing about what happened in Belstone Lane, so my evidence was superfluous and they didn't wish to put me to the trouble. There were two trials, were there not – first the so-called Payday Gang then your client and another, years later?

It was my turn to shake my head. 'There were three trials,' I said. 'The Payday Gang, where the jury couldn't find a verdict, and six years later my client and his friend, but in between three other men were tried for conspiracy to rob and acquitted. You knew nothing of that?'

'You do surprise me, Mr Tyroll, but being out of the West Midlands we don't see the news from there. Who were they?'

'Their names wouldn't mean anything,' I said, 'but they were all black.'

I owed Miss Callington my thanks but still it was nice to see her startled expression.

32

The ugly pre-war pub on the corner was empty, gutted by fire. Kids had torn off the protective boarding at the windows so as to use the shell for a fornicatorium or drug supermarket. The rest of the estate was little better, ravaged by six decades of municipal neglect and its occupants. None of it did anything for my mood.

A cab dropped Sheila and me one street away from the ruined pub. We stood outside a four-square, semi-detached pair of 1930s council houses. Billy Simpson's parents lived in the one on the right.

Mrs Simpson answered the doorbell. She was a stocky

old lady with a stoop and moved slowly along the hallway in front of us, guiding us to a big rectangular sitting-room where her husband sat in a corner armchair, staring at a television set. He was a plump, balding man with a pasty complexion which I guessed came from many days and nights of television. He rose stiffly and switched it off as we entered, a courtesy from another age.

'Mr Tyroll?' he said. 'Sit you down. Mary'll get some tea.'

We sat, and I wondered how to begin. This interview was always going to be difficult – before I knew that Billy had planned the Belstone Lane job. I looked around me for inspiration, seeking neutral ground on which to open the conversation. The ashtray by Simpson's chair was empty and clean, though he was finishing one cigarette and lighting another. The room had been prepared for visitors, made clean to propitiate strangers so that they would not bring bad news. On the tiled mantelpiece stood a colour photograph of a slim-faced young man giving the camera a wide smirk.

'Billy?' I asked, nodding towards it, though I well knew it was him.

'Ah,' said his father. He picked up the photograph and gazed at it before replacing it, then lowered himself back into his chair. 'What was it you wanted to know about him? And why now, after all this time?'

He wasn't going to cut me any slack, so I took a breath and started. First I explained my position, as I had already explained it to his wife on the phone. He heard me out in silence, his eyes never showing any response, and remained silent for a moment after I'd finished.

'You're not for Grady, are you?' he demanded at last.

'No,' I said. 'I represent Alan Walton only.'

'Alan's a good lad. Him and Billy was mates from kids, at school and all, but Grady said as Billy done it, killed that poor bloody guard and crippled his mate,' he said.

'Peter Grady has always said that his statement was forged by the police,' I said, 'and I believe him.'

His eyes narrowed, his chin came up and I knew he was going to ask the question I couldn't answer truthfully.

'Do you think he done it – our Billy?' he asked.

'Mr Simpson,' I said picking my words carefully, 'since Christmas I've read every word of the evidence that was put forward when Grady and my client were tried. I've been down Belstone Lane and talked to all the witnesses. I've spent hours with Alan Walton.'

'And . . . ?' he interrupted, sensing that I was hedging.

'There's nothing, nothing at all, in anything I've read that makes any kind of case against Billy. If they'd charged him he should have been acquitted.'

'And what about Alan and Grady?' he demanded. 'How was they convicted, then? What good evidence was there against them?'

'The forged confession by Grady and, of course, Glenys's evidence.'

'And she'd have done for him the same way she done for them,' he shot back. 'That's what she wanted – they didn't matter to her, it was our Billy she wanted and he knew it. That's why he did what he did, 'cause he wouldn't have stood going inside the way Alan and Grady have.'

He paused and narrowed his gaze again. 'So it was her and the police that sent Grady and Alan down, was it? There warn't no other evidence?'

'No,' I said, truthfully.

He nodded slowly and looked up at his son's picture. 'I knew there couldn't be,' he said. 'Now, what was it you wanted to know, Mr Tyroll?'

'About Glenys, mainly,' I said. 'I don't understand why she went to the police. However much she hated your son, it was all over, they were divorced.'

He shook his head. 'It warn't all over for her,' he said.

'She chased after our Billy in the first place and then she didn't like what she got. She took up with other chaps – '

I interrupted. 'Do you remember who any of those chaps were?'

He laughed, humourlessly. 'Now you're asking,' he said. 'She had lots of them, Mr Tyroll. Long before they ever broke up she was at it every night nearly. There wasn't so many night-clubs then, but she found places to go. She'd be up at the Kernel at Newtown, in the Spider's Web at Walsall, over in Brum, night after night. I don't know who she'd have been with,' and he shook his head.

'Do you know where she is now?' I asked.

'You won't find her,' said Mrs Simpson's voice behind me. 'She's gone.'

She had brought a tea-tray in and now set about serving us from the coffee table. 'She's long gone,' she repeated as she passed the cups.

'Gone?' I said. 'You mean left Belston, not – '

'Oh no! Not her!' she interrupted. 'Her sort take a while to go to the devil. She went down south, years ago.'

'Are you sure?' I asked. 'Do you know where she went?'

'I'm sure she went,' she said, 'but I don't know where. She might have said, but if she did it didn't sink in.'

'You talked to her?'

'Oh, yes. After the divorce and that we had no more to do with her. I'd always warned Billy against her, anyway. Then she went to the police and told her lies and after Billy was gone I could have killed her with my own hands. But I never saw her, until one day in the post office. I was just coming out as she was going in and she said, "Hello, Mary," bold as brass. Well, I wouldn't have said a word, but when she said that I said, "Who do you think you are, to call me by name?" '

'What did she say?'

'She said, "Look, Mrs Simpson, just because Billy and I were divorced doesn't mean we have to be unpleasant to each other." I said, "Divorced? The best day's work Billy ever done was getting divorced, like the worst was getting wed to you. But that's not it," I said. "You murdered my Billy, as sure as if you'd shot him dead. You and your lies!" '

The stocky little woman had straightened unconsciously as she recited her tale and I could imagine her planted foursquare on the pavement in front of Glenys, determined to say her piece.

'She stopped being smarmy then, and she turned nasty. "Well," she said, "if that's the way of it, I shan't be bothering you again," and that's when she said she was going away, down south somewhere. I said, "And which of your fancy chaps is paying for that or are they all chipping in?" '

We couldn't help it. We chuckled, and Mrs Simpson smiled at the memory of her thrust. 'She didn't like that. She said, "It might interest you to know that I got half the insurance reward for telling the truth about Billy and his mates." And with that she turned her back and went off and I ay seen her since.'

'The insurance reward?' I said. 'But the money from Belstone Lane was never recovered. There wouldn't have been a reward.'

'I don't know,' she said, 'but I know that's what she said. I told Arnold when I came home. We was furious.'

I couldn't make head or tail of that, but it was clearly the case that Glenys had disappeared. We finished our tea and Mr Simpson called us a cab. His wife escorted us to the door.

As I shook her hand she leaned forward and said, 'I'm glad you came, Mr Tyroll. You told Arnold just what he wanted to hear.' I still don't know if that meant what I think it did.

33

Claude was in the office next morning. I told him that Glenys Simpson was a waste of his time, that she was gone. As an afterthought I asked him to work his insurance connections and find out if any kind of reward had been paid on the Belstone Lane case. If Glenys really did have half the reward, I wanted to know who had the other half.

Then I phoned Grady's solicitor. Without Legal Aid or private funds, he was unable to do anything with his client's case.

'Tell me,' I asked him, 'you didn't ever get Grady's alleged confession statement ESDA tested, did you?'

'No,' he said. 'If we'd got through the first hurdle in the Court of Appeal and had our Legal Aid Order renewed, I was going to do that, obviously. Why do you ask?'

'Because I'm pretty certain now as to who carried out the Belstone Lane job, so your man's statement must be a fake. Get it ESDA'd and charge it to me. My client will pay.'

Out of the whole mess I had at last established a fact – that the Trumans robbed the Mantons van and killed the driver's mate. Now, perhaps, there was a chance of doing Alan Walton some good. Still a little whisper reminded me of Alasdair's analysis – that the significant pattern was the repeated failures of the police – and I still couldn't explain those.

Jayne my faithful secretary stuck her head round the door. She had been with me ever since I set up my own practice, graduating from a rickety desk with an old upright typewriter to the latest and glossiest of word-processors.

Apart from her typing skills, she imposed order on drunks in the waiting-room with a single flash of her eyes, found long-lost files, buttered up angry clients and ordered me and Alasdair about.

'There's a lady in the waiting-room with an insurance problem,' she said, 'but there's no one to see her – unless you will.'

She looked at me with an expression that dared me to turn away the business.

I was beginning to feel good about Walton's case, so I gave in gracefully. 'Send her in,' I said. 'Send her in.'

Mrs Treasure White was black, in her late thirties, strikingly attractive and knew it.

'What can I do for you, Mrs White?' I asked.

'Well, you see, my brother died and he made a will for me to have everything of his.'

I nodded.

'Now, he didn't have much, but when we was small our mother had insurances on us. I don't suppose it's very big, but I know Momma paid it all up and I should be entitled to it.'

'So what's the difficulty? Have you been in touch with the insurance company?'

'Well, I came down from Manchester for my brother's funeral and I brought the insurance papers that I had from Momma and I went to the brokers who fixed it all up for Momma when we lived in Belston.'

'What did they say?'

'They weren't much good. They said I'd have to prove he was dead and prove that I was his next-of-kin and so on. I don't think they wanted to know, Mr Tyroll.'

I nodded. 'Insurance brokers make their money selling policies for insurance companies. They don't make anything out of helping people to claim against insurers.'

She smiled. 'The people I'm staying with here in Belston said I should get a lawyer and they said you was good.'

'Kind of them,' I said. 'But it shouldn't be much trouble.'

I reached for a green Legal Advice form and started to fill it in. That done I began collecting particulars from her. The penny only dropped when I asked her if she'd got a copy of her brother's death certificate. She produced one from her handbag and passed it across.

George Cook, with an address on Wolverhampton Road, murdered – she was Banjo Cook's sister! With a few questions I established that she had married Benjamin White's younger brother and was now divorced from him. I could scarcely contain myself but I managed to go on jotting down particulars, dictated the necessary letters, explained what would happen and buzzed Jayne to organise coffee for me and my new client.

'I've done all that needs doing for the moment,' I said, 'and I don't imagine there will be any problem. Eventually we'll get the money out of them, but there's something else, something where you may be able to help me.'

She looked surprised.

'Obviously,' I said, 'you know how your brother died.' She nodded. 'What you probably don't know is that I was the person who found him.'

Her eyes widened. 'You were?' she said.

'Yes, Mrs White. I had gone to Bert's Café to interview your brother.'

She looked cautious. 'What was that about?'

'About something that happened a long time ago – about the Belstone Lane robbery.'

I had been watching her closely and I saw it – the flicker of reaction before she suppressed it.

'What was that?' she said as though she had never heard of it.

'It was the armed robbery of a security van, Mrs White, in which one guard died and another was crippled.'

Again the slight flicker. 'I don't know why you should think George would know about that,' she said.

'Let's stop beating about the bush,' I said. 'Your brother

is dead. Nothing I do can harm him but if he'd lived he might have been able to help me and a client of mine.'

I told her Alan Walton's story while she sipped her coffee and said nothing. When I had done she put the cup down and looked sideways at the wall for a long time. Then she shook her head.

'He wouldn't have helped you, Mr Tyroll. He was my own brother and he's gone, but he wouldn't have helped you. Georgy only did things for money. Anything – bad things.'

She picked up the cup again and spoke across its top. 'He was a bad man, Mr Tyroll. That's why we went to Manchester – to get away from him.'

'How was he bad?' I asked.

'When he was a boy he started smoking ganja – you know, cannabis? But that wasn't enough for him. He started on other things and he couldn't stop. Then he never had enough money. He stole off everybody, he stole off me, he stole off Momma. He started going with crooks, like the Truman brothers. Then he got caught.'

She looked me in the eyes. 'You don't let down your own, do you, Mr Tyroll? But Georgy did. When the police caught him he gave up his friends for money. It got so he couldn't buy drugs in the Midlands, he had to go to London, because people was afraid to do business with him.'

'Who was the policeman?' I asked, crossing my fingers under the desk.

She shook her head slowly. 'I don't know,' she said. 'He was a big man. Most times he'd give Georgy money for names, but sometimes he'd give Georgy drugs and let him deal. Then the policeman would take money from Georgy. He used to come round late on a Friday night and sit out in his car.'

'What was he like?'

'He was big, tall and he dressed very well. Too good for

a policeman. And he wore spectacles, not proper shades, but tinted like.'

Hawkins! I picked up the Walton file and riffled through the photocopies of newspaper items at the back. One was an obituary of Hawkins. I pulled it out and showed her the photograph.

'That's the man,' she said, without hesitation. 'That's him.'

'Do you know anything about the Belstone Lane robbery?' I asked quietly.

A weary look passed across her face. 'I know about it, Mr Tyroll. Georgy was there and the Trumans and my stupid brother-in-law.'

'What happened to the money? I've been told that your brother had it all.'

She shook her head again. 'Oh no!' she said. 'He thought he was going to have a big share, but Mr Big – your policeman there – he had most of it. Georgy only got a little bit.'

'Didn't the others complain?'

'Oh, yes! They complained at Georgy. That was when they got arrested. After that they didn't complain no more. They went away.'

'Where did they go? I've been looking for them.'

She smiled. 'You won't find them, Mr Tyroll. Not in this country. Do you need to find them?'

'Not really, Mrs White. In the light of what you have told me, they're not going to speak if I do find them, or they're not going to tell the truth. I'm grateful to you and so will my client be – I hope.'

She stood up. 'I hope that helps your man in prison, Mr Tyroll, but I think that's all I can tell you about poor Georgy.'

She turned back at the door. 'I would have spoken up before,' she said, 'but I never knew. After the boys was acquitted that was it. I went to Manchester and I tried to put it all away.'

I saw her out and returned to my desk. I picked up the obituary cutting and looked at Hawkins' big head with the narrow-framed, tinted glasses – Mr Big! Now I understood the police failures to catch the Belstone Lane killers.

Something in the text caught my eye. I read on. At one point I had wondered how Hawkins had died and here it was, lying unnoticed in my file. He had indeed dropped dead in his garden from a heart attack, but not alone. He had been drinking with two old chums – Watters and Saffary! Had they shared the loot? Of course they would have done. They were as thick as – as thick as thieves. Had they fallen out? Had one of them slipped him a deadly Mickey in his lager? I guessed I'd never know.

34

I was almost there. If Peter Grady's solicitor got a good ESDA report on the statement – if it was a provable fake – we were home and dry. We could go back to the Court of Appeal with a chance. I hoped.

I kept Treasure White's information to myself, waiting to see the ESDA report and reveal to the world what a clever boy I was. Sheila turned sarcastic about the 'I know something you don't know' looks that she detected on my face occasionally but she was up to something as well. There were a lot of phone calls to London and a couple to Sydney which she passed off as 'research'. I was too excited to pay much attention.

The report on Grady's statement reached me within days. It was all that I had hoped for. It even confirmed what Hughes had told me:

> Not only does the evidence show that the pages of Exhibit GH/2 were written out of sequence, Page 3 has

an impression on it of an alternative version of Page 5, implying that there may have been several 'dummy runs' at creating the desired text or that there was more than one version of the document.

Jayne came in and caught me skipping round the room with the report in my hands.

'Good news!' I said. 'I was just a little bit excited.'

She fixed me with a cold eye. 'Well, ah,' she said.

I invited Alasdair, John Parry, Claude and Mac to dine. Mac was there by way of an apology for abusing his friendship. Once again we settled down with the whisky after dinner.

'Well come on, then, bach,' urged Parry. 'You've been going about for days looking like the cat that got the cream. What's on?'

I lowered my glass solemnly on to the coffee table and leaned forward. 'I have solved', I said, 'the mystery of the Belstone Lane robbery.'

That caught the audience. Sheila mouthed 'Ratbag!' silently at me, but the others waited my explanation.

'Firstly,' I began, 'Billy Simpson augmented his income by spotting opportunities and planning jobs for the Pay-day Gang. One of his ideas was the Mantons van which was begging for it, always using Belstone Lane to go to Bellsich. But the Payday Gang didn't fancy it, so he offered it to Banjo Cook.'

'Did he know that Cook was a police informer?' asked Sheila.

'I guess not. It'd have been pretty silly if he did. But Cook went to his mentor – Mr Big, Chief Inspector Hawkins – and Hawkins saw a chance to make some real money. So he let the job go ahead, certain that it would be blamed on the Payday Gang. But it all went pear-shaped and there was a killing.'

'It makes sense,' said Sheila. 'Remember we thought that Grady might have been there because his statement referred to a woman screaming – either that or the police who forged the statement knew what had happened in Belstone Lane.'

I nodded and took a drink. 'Hawkins was nothing if not an opportunist. Once there was a killing in the picture and life sentences in the offing he knew that nobody could fall out about the robbery. So he swiped the loot and when the Trumans started to grumble about it, he let them have a little taste of being on trial just to shut them up. It worked – when they were acquitted they went abroad.'

'But at that point,' said Alasdair, 'he'd got it made. He'd got away with the loot. He'd side-tracked Miss Callington, the one witness who knew that it was a black gang that robbed the Mantons van, and he'd frightened Cook and the Trumans off. So why mess with Walton and Grady?'

'Good question,' I said, 'and I can only guess the answer.'

'Here we go,' said Parry, 'lawyer's guesswork. It's no substitute for evidence, you know.'

'Nevertheless,' I said, 'it fits. When Billy Simpson found his wife was having a long-term affair with somebody, he used his intercom thing to bug the sitting-room and tape their conversation and he told his mates he knew who the boyfriend was.'

'And he was a fellow who liked to score off his enemies,' said Macintyre, 'so he was going to do something about it.'

'Right!' I said. 'Now – I believe he let his wife know that he'd identified her boyfriend.'

'And who was the boyfriend?' asked Alasdair.

'Hawkins,' I said. 'She told him that Billy had rumbled them. Hawkins couldn't take a chance – Simpson might know about his connection with Banjo Cook as well. Billy Simpson had to be stopped.'

'Why didn't he just arrest him for the robbery?' asked Sheila.

'Because Billy Simpson was deadly dangerous. If he could connect Cook and Hawkins he just might have done it in court. So Billy Simpson had to be neutralised and the Belstone Lane job laid to rest for ever and here was the lovely Glenys, a tool ready to hand, willing to put her husband and his mates away for Hawkins' sake.'

'You said "neutralised",' said Parry. 'Did you mean "killed"?'

'I don't know. Perhaps Hawkins had him killed. I think that's likely. But perhaps Billy caught on that he could only get his pals out of trouble by getting himself and another bunch of pals into it. Maybe he topped himself. I don't know.'

'But why Walton and Grady?' said Alasdair.

'That's easy. Because they were close mates of Billy Simpson, and because Saffary hates Walton. So they leaned on all of them and finally it worked. Grady cracked, signed a fake confession, and it was enough to nail both of them.'

'Why does Saffary hate Walton?' Sheila asked.

'That's another thing I don't know.'

'Ha!' snorted the big Welshman. 'This remarkable solution has slid from lawyer's imaginings to "don't knows". It's not worth the paper it's not written on!'

I thought he was serious for a moment, and it brought me up short. Then he grinned.

'I', he said, 'can now reveal the truth about Saffary's down on Walton. I have been hanging about police clubs and other unsavoury locations, keeping my big copper's ears flapping.'

'Well, fire away, old cock,' said Alasdair.

'Less of the old,' said Parry. 'Saffary, as you know, has certain personality problems, only one of which is drink. Just when he was about to be raised to the dizzy heights of an inspectorship, than which there is no greater honour, he fell from grace. What's more, he was caught – bang to rights, as they say in the cheap novels.'

'What happened?' I asked.

'Somebody sent the chief superintendent a photograph of . . .'

'. . . Saffary and his mates, piling out of the back door of a pub into a police car,' I finished for him. 'But it wasn't Walton who sent that!'

'There was an anonymous letter with it, referring to Walton's conviction.'

'So there was, but it was Billy Simpson who sent it!'

'Duw, duw,' said Parry. 'You mean that Saffary's been wasting his malice on the wrong man?'

'I'm afraid so. He also jailed the wrong man.'

'That never bothers him,' said Parry.

I shook my head and returned to my explanation.

'Anyway,' I said, 'everything had worked, Simpson was out of the way, the Trumans had vanished, Hawkins – and Watters and Saffary, no doubt – had the loot, and Grady and Walton were inside. Then Walton appealed again so Hawkins admits to his bosses that there's been a bit of corner-cutting, and that's all right, they don't mind a bit of lying to the Court of Appeal to cover up over-enthusiasm in a senior officer, so it's all right again until little Mrs Cassidy bungs a carrier bag on my desk and asks me to spring her son-in-law. Then it's open season on Banjo Cook and appellants' lawyers.'

Parry was shaking his big head slowly. 'Very good,' he said. 'Lovely, in fact. All fits together, doesn't it? But it rather depends on whether Hawkins and Glenys really were lovers, and you can't prove that. You can't find her, and if you do, she's a hard case – she's not going to burst into tears and say, "Yes, we dunnit! My lover Gerry Hawkins and I conspired to frame two men!" Not likely, is it?'

It was the weak point. I had a good guess, but no evidence. I couldn't answer.

Claude intervened. 'Might I have a word?'

'Ha!' snorted Parry. 'I wondered when we'd hear from the gentleman amateurs.'

Claude grinned. 'If you don't want early retirement and a fat pension, John, I'll take you on any day. Then you can spend your old age tramping round housing estates in the rain and getting arrested by the duly authorised forces of law and order.'

'No, no, bach. You speak your piece. We have to allow a little licence for imagination now and then.'

Claude pulled a notebook from his pocket and glanced at a page. 'Hawkins', he said, 'made personal representations to the insurers that, although the loot had not been recovered, there was a point of principle – that without Glenys coming forward there would have been no convictions. Therefore they should pay a reward to discourage future robbers. So they did – to Glenys.'

Everyone stared. Claude went on, 'He even persuaded Mantons to fork out a bit extra.'

Parry broke the silence that followed. 'I apologise,' he said. 'So you've got your story. Glenys and Hawkins split the reward. What are you going to do about it now?'

'Reinstate Walton's appeal – and Grady's.'

'Fine, fine,' he said. 'And having put forward an explanation which, filled with lawyer's guesses and "don't knows" as it was, is probably what happened, what do I do about it?'

'You?' said Sheila.

'Me,' he said. 'I am a police officer ever alert to protect society from the forces that threaten to destroy it and Christopher here has just given me a plausible outline of a conspiracy to rob and murder. You can probably make your case in the Court of Appeal – "unsafe and unsatisfactory" and all that – but where do I go, looking for evidence "beyond reasonable doubt"?'

I smiled. 'Try this,' I said, and took a cassette from my pocket.

He took it and stared at it. 'What's this?' he said, suspiciously.

'You remember I gave you the tape of the threatening phone call?'

He nodded. 'Not much use unless we had a voice to compare it with.'

'There's the voice,' I said. 'That's a recording of an interview on the phone with Desmond Murphy – former Central Crime Squad officer, pal of Hawkins, he calls him "Gerry", and erstwhile security manager for Mantons who also happens to be the man who made the threatening call.'

Parry's eyes were wide. 'You're absolutely certain sure?' he said.

I nodded. 'Put that and the threatening call through a voice analysis and then go and see Mr Murphy and ask him about Hawkins and Belstone Lane. Unless he wants to be tied to the killings, he'll talk.'

35

Murphy talked. He talked loudly enough for charges to be made. Watters and Saffary were arrested and the week before the reinstated appeal of Alan Walton and Peter Grady was heard by the Court of Appeal, I walked across Jubilee Square to see the newspaper boards – 'CENTRAL OFFICERS CHARGED'. I made a point of being in the Magistrates' Court the next morning to see them remanded in custody and to make sure that Saffary saw me watching. I owed him at least that.

It was only days before the Court of Appeal hearing. The arrests of the two CID officers had been a clear signal that we no longer had anything to worry about. All of a sudden life looked bright again and, as though in sympathy, the weather improved. Sleet and snow gave way to sunny days, cold but cheerful after the weeks of darkness and